W9-AHY-113

DEVIL'S WIND

DEVIL'S WIND

DOUGLAS HIRT

A Double D Western
Doubleday
NEW YORK LONDON TORONTO SYDNEY AUCKLAND

A Double D Western
Published by Doubleday, a division of
Bantam Doubleday Dell Publishing Group, Inc.,
666 Fifth Avenue, New York, New York 10103.

A Double D Western, Doubleday, and the portrayal of the letters DD are trademarks of Doubleday, a division of Bantam Doubleday Dell Publishing Group, Inc.

All of the characters in this book are fictitious, and any resemblance to actual persons, living or dead, is purely coincidental.

Library of Congress Cataloging-in-Publication Data
Hirt, Douglas.
Devil's wind.
(Double D western)
I. Title.
PS3558.I727D47 1989 813'.54 88-3733
ISBN 0-385-23756-1
Copyright © 1989 by Douglas Hirt
All Rights Reserved
Printed in the United States of America
February 1989
First Edition
OG

To Kathryn;
my wife, my friend

DEVIL'S WIND

1

They stood over the open graves like statues in a musty museum; motionless but for the heaving and sobbing which rose as a bitter wail on the sad evening air. The odor of smoldering wood was an evil incense; it so permeated the little village, seeping under closed doors and through broken windows, that they no longer noticed it. Even the dogs that ran so freely just two days earlier now sensed the change which had spread its dark shroud over their masters; some lay curled and whimpering against cool adobe walls, others slinked in silence, tails drawn up and heads low to the ground.

The people—those who remained—looked down upon the freshly dug holes, thirteen in number with thirteen crudely fitted wooden boxes waiting to be covered. Onesimo Gutiérrez had been a close friend of the priest; an honest, hardworking man in his own humble way and a strongly active church member. At Christmas time or during the Easter season or the Feast of the Immaculate Conception it was always Onesimo who would make the preparations and see to it that everyone in the little village of San Pablo had either a chore to perform or a part to play in the season pageant . . . Now it was Onesimo they all chose for this ceremony.

Onesimo took a little handful of dirt from each grave, sprinkling it on the boxes and allowing the tears to roll freely down his fat, sunburned cheeks as he spoke the name of each one in a soft voice. At the end he opened the priest's Bible, which they had somehow miraculously recovered from the flames of the church, and read the passages the good Father had circled in pencil for just such an occasion. Had it been a wedding feast instead of a funeral they could have just as easily located other passages similarly circled, for the Father had been a precise man who left very little to chance or caprice; it was an easy chore for Onesimo to find just the right words to say now.

When he had finished, his eyes turned to heaven; the sun had dropped below the horizon, turning the sky bloodred. *Christ's blood,* he thought, shed for our sins and the sins of our little ones. Another tear. Onesimo knew that the good Savior above was also crying with them . . . and for the priest. With teary eyes lifted, he began the Lord's Prayer; they all whispered it together. As they spoke the final Amen, Onesimo returned to his wife's side. Her eyes too were red, her face streaked, and she looked as if the ordeal had aged her a dozen years.

Rosina took Onesimo's arm. "It should have been the priest to lay our children and friends to rest," she said, "to give their souls into the hand of God."

"Sí," he answered softly, looking up at the blackened walls of the church. In places, where the fire had burned through the vigas, the roof had collapsed and the second floor of the church had fallen in upon itself. *"Sí,* Rosina," he said again in a voice heavy with pain. "But we have no priest now."

Rosina's fingers tightened around her husband's arm and

her eyes turned down to the graves. She said, "It would be a blessing if one of them was Juana."

At the sound of his daughter's name Onesimo began to sob openly. His old frame shuddered as he thought of the men who had done this, who had carried her away—the evil men with their wicked desires! Yes, it would have been better if Juana had been counted among the dead. At least then they would know of her fate—the not knowing was an ache in their hearts harder to bear than death.

They all cried as the light faded away. They cried for their children, for their friends, for the priest and for themselves; it was well after dark before the broken families began to return to their homes to console each other in their grief.

But tomorrow would be another day; tomorrow the fields would have to be replanted, tomorrow they would have to pick up the pieces of their lives and put them back together —tomorrow life would have to begin again and maybe, someday, they would be able to rebuild their beloved church where cool ivy once grew green along the garden wall and the water ran free and happy.

It was a black day for San Pablo, that day in August 1898, a day they would all remember far too long.

2

Simmering under a noonday sun, the Sonoran Desert was the pit of the Devil's hell; a windless, sweltering furnace where waves of quivering heat climbed off great sandstone boulders and choked the wide, tan stretches of baking sand.

Matt Kendell squinted under the wide brim of his sweat-soaked hat, raising the flat of his hand to shade his eyes from the evil sun. There, in the distance, shimmering on the horizon like a dancing mirage on some vast waterless plain, lay the Dragoon Mountains, and between him and the coolness of those mountains stretched thirty miles of searing wasteland, prickly mesquite, sage and rattlesnakes.

The cloudless sky above was white hot and the sand beneath his horse's hooves a potter's kiln, and somewhere between that burning sky and baked sand—between him and the Dragoons—Kendell knew he would find them. He would find them if he had to scour every damned inch of hell . . . he would find them.

A buzzard soared effortlessly overhead in a long, lazy spiral on the heat rising off the desert floor. Kendell watched it swing away, feeling somehow akin to the ugly bird. It too was living out a hell of sorts on the high Sonoran—Kendell had his own hell to contend with.

The horse shifted on the hot sand. Kendell stroked the animal's ears and dismounted, filled his hat from the water bag and offered the drink to the animal. The hat was cool when he tugged it back onto his head and he took a short drink from the water bag. The water had to be rationed and the horse needed it as badly as he—perhaps more so considering it was doing all the work at the moment.

Another lonely bird swung overhead. Kendell lifted himself into the saddle and winced as the stabbing pain cut into his side. Red was spreading again across the already crusted shirt. Pressing a hand onto the wound, he straightened slowly in the saddle. It needed time to heal properly. He knew that, but time was a luxury he could not allow himself. The pain eased after a while and he got the horse moving again.

Soft sand slowed him, but then it would be slowing them too; everything was equal, he told himself, or at least he would make it all equal when he caught up with them. The thought of vengeance consumed him like a fire; it urged him on, paling the other pains—the pain in his side . . . the pain in his heart—into insignificance.

Stories say a white man cannot cross these lands, that the Indians only knew of the secret watering places—those which weren't alkali. Kendell had heard the stories and never paid them much mind. He had had other things to contend his soul and for many years adventuring had not been one of them. Now he tried desperately to recall them.

It was the Chiricahua Apache who used to call this hell their home before President Grant made his treaty with Cochise, in 1872, setting aside the Chiricahua Reservation. It had been in the Dragoon Mountains that General Oliver O. Howard had finally been allowed to meet with Cochise and negotiate the treaty. Tom Jeffords had been instrumental in the negotiations of the treaty, which, like most other treaties, lasted only a few years. Kendell seemed to recall the year 1876—two years after the death of Cochise—that was when the government rescinded the treaty and packed the whole Chiricahua nation off to San Carlos. Well, almost the whole nation. Kendell was aware that even to this day bands of Apaches still roamed; angry men who could not accept the present, who lived in the past and thought raiding and murdering innocent whites would somehow change things, would somehow bring back their proud past.

The past, Kendell scoffed, and it brought a foul taste to his mouth. No one can bring back the past! Until this very moment he had never really known what those few renegades had been fighting for. Now the reality of it struck him. A stunning revelation. They say a man must walk in another's boots to truly understand. Matt Kendell was beginning to understand the vengeance which drove those Indians who were clinging to a past that no longer existed, and, suddenly, like the ugly birds passing overhead, he knew a certain kinship with them, too.

He occupied himself with these thoughts through the long, hot hours—the proper time for crossing this desert was after dark, but of late nothing in his life had been very proper. Glancing again at that terrible sun, he might have asked God for guidance except the God he once knew had deserted him—if indeed He had ever existed.

3

Four men dismounted and took their horses into the shade of a low ridge. The three women remained in the sun, hands tied with leather thongs to their saddles. Pedro tugged off the heavy pack and let the mule wander away. The grass here was sparse and dry as straw but it was sufficient for the animal's needs.

Jake Sargot squatted in the shade, removing his hat and allowing the hot air to cool the sweat on his brow and bald head. His cheeks burned red above the coarse black beard. "It will be better tomorrow," he said, squinting out at the harsh landscape.

Pedro laughed briefly. "No, not tomorrow nor the next day. August is never a good month in this desert."

"The water is almost gone, Jake," Ben Jones noted, lifting the skins from his saddle. "I sure as hell hope you know what you're doing."

"I know what I'm doing, damn it," Sargot said, narrowing an eye at the skinny man. "You want to turn around and head back, you better do it now. Once we reach those mountains nobody turns back."

"I didn't mean that, Jake. It's just that we're running low, we didn't figure on them." He nodded at the three women waiting in the sun.

"I know what I'm doing," Sargot said, glancing at the Apache, who was sitting cross-legged in the shadow of a boulder and handing up clumps of buffalo grass to his horse. The old Indian felt Sargot's eyes upon him, paused and looked back at the bearded man across the glaring sand.

"The Apache knows the places," Sargot said, turning away.

Jones took the water skins to the three in the sun and gave each a drink. Sargot returned his gaze to the bleak horizon shimmering in the heat. The Apache's black eyes moved across the landscape, too. They were unrevealing eyes, wary as a fox, wise as an old owl; eyes which saw many things and in a moment they paused and lingered along the trail which their horses had left coming down from the north. Cuchillo Rojo would have smiled had it been his nature to do so. Just the same, inwardly he knew a certain twinge of satisfaction which his tired old heart could not explain; something had appealed to his savage heart. He rose slowly and went to Sargot.

Sargot looked up. "What is it?" he asked.

Cuchillo hunched down beside the big man and nodded his head toward the women. "It is not good they stay in the sun too long."

"The hell, let 'em fry."

Cuchillo studied Sargot's eyes; hard, unfeeling, with lines etched deep into the dry skin surrounding them. His head was bald and pink where the hat protected it and the wild beard that hid his face looked out of place beneath the Sonoran sun. Cuchillo had seen men such as this before, up in the high mountains where the air was always cool, but down in the desert, his home, such men were rare. He turned his eyes toward the Dragoon Mountains.

"The mountains and the place you want to go to are still

two days' ride. The women, they can take the heat, but the horses, they cannot. Tired horses slow us down, maybe a day, maybe more. I would not speak of this now but for a thing you must know."

The Apache paused and Sargot looked at him. "What thing?"

Cuchillo's eyes lifted and stared down their trail. "We are being followed."

"Followed?" Sargot rose to his feet and nodded his head toward the dusty land which stretched to the horizon. "Who can follow us across that hellhole?"

Cuchillo shrugged his shoulders. "This I do not know." He looked hard at Sargot. "I think it must be the Evil One, the one your people call the Devil."

"The Devil?" He glared down at Cuchillo. "What the hell makes you think we're being followed?"

Cuchillo shook his head. "I just know. I feel him drawing near. Sometimes, when I look at the desert where the sky reaches down to touch it, his voice whispers to me on the wind. It says, 'I come now.' I do not know who he is, only that he comes, and the Evil One rides with him."

"That's just Indian superstition crap," Sargot said flatly. He strode away a few paces then turned. "Are you certain?"

Cuchillo nodded.

"Then we better make tracks."

"No." Cuchillo gazed off to the east, his eyes studying something the others did not see. "No, he will not come today—he will come, but not this day. It is better we rest and wait for night, then we can continue. It is better now to go by night," he said and his eyes remained fixed on a distant point.

Sargot weighed the Indian's words. "All right, we'll wait," and there was an unusual note of reluctance in his voice. He turned to Ben Jones. "Untie them women and bring the horses into the shade." Turning back to Cuchillo, he added, "You better be right about this."

Ben Jones brought the horses in and removed the straps binding the women's hands and feet, stepping back as they climbed stiffly to the ground. His fingers flexed convulsively about the hilt of a long knife he wore at his side and his lips curled in an uncontrolled grin. Drawing the blade, he prodded the women against the rocks then lashed their hands together, stepping back and wiping his sweaty palms across his vest. He stared at them with wide, greedy eyes.

"Which one of you tonight?" he said, dragging an arm across his cracked lips. "Huh? How 'bout you, pretty one—though I can say for certain you ain't so pretty now as you was two days ago, but you'll do, all right."

The girl glared back at him through eyes hardened with hate, but she held her tongue. They had all learned early on these were not men of patience. Jones stretched out his hand, resting it upon her trembling neck, feeling with pleasure her small body cringe beneath his fingers.

"Hell," he said, suddenly thrusting the knife back into its sheath, "there ain't no reason why we have to wait till night," and he untied her hands.

Sargot's fingers dug into his narrow shoulders and threw him to the ground.

"That one's mine," he said, stepping between Jones and the girl, his hand coming to rest on the pistol at his side. "You keep hands off or you'll go through the rest of your natural life tweeting like a bird."

Jones regained his feet, staring uneasily into the wide, hairy face confronting him. "What you want to go and divvy 'em up for, Jake? I just figured we use 'em between us."

"You figured wrong, Ben. I want that one. Do what you like with the others, I don't care."

Pedro wandered over and Sargot said to the both of them, "You two can fight over them and I won't give two hoots in hell, but the one on the end is mine and I'll bury the man who thinks otherwise." He looked back at the young girl. Her olive-colored skin was dirty, her face streaked and the long black hair that hung across dark, wide eyes was knotted and greasy now. The long skirt she wore was torn and smudged and the sturdy white blouse was ripped down its front. Despite the weary, bedraggled figure she cut, Jake Sargot liked what he saw there, and if Jake Sargot liked something, Jake Sargot made it his. That's the way it was, that's the way it had always been—the way it would always be.

He returned his attention to Pedro and Jones, saw their hungry looks and knew he could take the both of them any time he pleased—but then it would just be him and the Apache, and now with riders coming up behind them those odds didn't look too appealing. He'd have time later to settle any score that needed settling. He'd take on any complaints about the way he was running things after they were safely into the Dragoons; after his trail was cold and the gold from the church safely stowed away—then he'd answer their stinks—but not now.

Sargot pushed a grin across his face and dropped his hand away from the gun. "Hell, I'll get tired of her in a week or two and then you'll have all three of them." He laughed and the tension eased back as he pushed past them and went down to where the Apache was sitting by his horse.

Ben Jones threw a hard look at Pedro and then to the girls huddling together. Whatever thoughts of frivolities he might have entertained a moment before were gone. Scooping up a handful of sand, he flung it at a nearby sage bush and sulked down to where his horse was nibbling at some dried grass.

Pedro went back to the spot of shade he had abandoned when all the trouble had started, pulled his hat over his eyes and let the hot afternoon worry the lizards and the scorpions and the rattlesnakes—it wasn't about to worry him. Pedro knew the desert well enough not to fight her. Before he fell asleep he recalled the words his father had spoken to him as a boy: "My son," his father had told him, "the desert is like a mighty wind that blows relentlessly; therefore, you must be like the willow that bends unceasingly."

Pedro was a very good willow.

4

Matt Kendell drew up, leaning forward in the saddle, listening. Riders were coming. He reined off the trail and moved behind the rise of a mesquite hummock, swinging out of the saddle. The wound spit fire into his side—something he had to ignore now as he drew the Winchester from its scabbard. Moving among the mesquite needles, which scratched painfully through his clothing, Kendell found a place to wait, out of sight, and in a moment the first riders appeared over a low ridge.

Chiricahua Apaches. He counted four of them . . . and a white woman. They were leading two riderless horses and it was just plain obvious that the white woman who accompanied them wasn't a captive, but appeared instead to be leading the party. Through the slender green leaves Kendell watched the party angling toward his hiding place.

They came on slowly, as if with no particular place to go and in no particular hurry to get there. At that moment Kendell wished he spoke Apache, for their words now meant nothing to him, but as they drew near it became clear it probably amounted to just so much idle chatter and bantering between a group of men. The white woman looked to be late in years and did not speak. She rode among the men in silence, but there was something about her eyes that disturbed him; the way they darted in an aimless fashion, as if only half aware of what they were seeing. Her dried lips puckered out in a peculiar manner too and her presence made Kendell vaguely uneasy in an unexplainable way . . . a way the presence of the Indians never could. It wasn't a feeling he could conveniently put his finger on—he wasn't even sure if it was real at all.

Kendell was aware that his side was bleeding again, maybe it had never stopped. He turned his hand over, staring at the blood on his fingers.

The Apaches were riding straight for him now; he had a sickening feeling in the pit of his stomach that this was the very place, of all the thousands of places exactly like it, where they were heading.

Perhaps one of them had seen him. Death by the hands of the Apache could be slow or fast and a lot depended on their mood at the time. Cochise had been a fair man and death at his hands would have been swift—but these renegades, well, that might be something else. Like himself, they had an ax to grind and death could be very slow coming. Somehow that notion didn't concern him. The thought which nettled him now, however, was that if he died his mission would be at an end, he'd never find *them.* He could not accept that fate and his fingers tightened around the rifle in his hand.

The lead man drew up, turned back to his friends and spoke a word in Apache, waving an arm in the air. It must have been something humorous because they all laughed. Suddenly the old woman commenced to cackling and a cautious mood swept over them.

"Pretty dress, heh?" she was saying, bobbing her head as she stared crazy-eyed at them. "Annie got pretty dress," she laughed, fingering the blue gingham of the sleeve. The garment was clean and feminine and looked sharply out of place on the back of this filthy, tangled old woman. Kendell decided it was all in what a person takes pride in. This grizzled woman was a mangy old crow, but she was still a woman and damn it, she was going to dress like one. Well, that was the impression, at least. She grinned at her Indian companions and said, "You want to kiss Annie now, heh, Injun boys, heh?"

They gave each other a smile and said something Kendell could not understand, chuckling among themselves. Annie cackled again and puckered up her swollen lips at them.

They waved her off laughing and she joined them with a screechy sound that shot through him like bare fingernails across a blackboard—then suddenly another sound riveted him.

It was a dry rattling at the roots of one of the bushes, and it made him think of a hollow gourd—but he knew it wasn't that at all. Without moving his body, Kendell swiveled an eye. The snake lay coiled there in the shade within an easy strike of his leg, its head held up on its thick body, swaying ever so slightly as if caught in a gentle breeze. Dark slit-eyes watched him and its tongue darted out, tasting him on the wind. Kendell's breath caught and stuck like a lump in his throat. It had to be the granddaddy of all rattlesnakes, thick as his wrist and at least six feet long stretched out—well, that was an estimation; Kendell had no great desire to verify it. Trying to keep tabs on the approaching Indians had suddenly become very difficult.

The hot desert sun had nothing to do with the sweat beading up on Kendell's cheeks as a quick look confirmed that, indeed, at least one of the riders had taken a particular interest in his little corner of the world. The Indian carried a bow with some arrows slung across his back, and except for that and a knife at his side, he was essentially unarmed —unarmed compared to Kendell's repeating rifle—but still deadly. Of the four, only one carried a rifle—an old caplock left over from the war—and the owner appeared to be the one in command. Now he spoke.

The man approaching Kendell stopped and swung his horse around. The one with the rifle was already sliding off his animal and dropping to his knees to examine the tracks in the sand.

He had only a moment as two other Indians climbed down from their horses to gather together over the tracks for a pow-wow, and now the rattles hissed like escaping steam while the snake's broad, flat head arched back. As far as snakes were concerned, Kendell did not think that they were especially noted for their patience—but then snakes had never been his specialty; he didn't much care for them when they were out of reach and he was certain he cared even less for the ones in striking distance. In some respects snakes were probably to blame for the sorry state of man today, but now he put that notion off, regretful he hadn't taken the time to learn some *real* facts about them instead of the cute little stories. At the moment he'd trade a hundred cute stories for one hard fact to use against the critter.

About all he could recall was that they were as unpredictable as everything else in this world, and somewhere he had heard that if a man freezes stone-still a rattlesnake wouldn't strike. It was mighty slim advice to depend on, but it was all he had.

He glanced quickly back to the Indians; the pow-wow

wasn't going to last forever . . . and neither was that snake's patience. Slowly tilting the barrel of his rifle around in front of him, he brought the barrel forward, presenting it to the snake, waving the round, blue-steel tube ever so slightly. In another second the snake was weaving back and forth in rhythm with its motion. Kendell held his breath, his eyes leaping from the snake to the Indians and back.

They were still jabbering excitedly.

It struck at the rifle, fangs lashing out like red-hot needles. For an instant it hung there clamped to the tube, amber fluid dripping onto the barrel; the next instant Kendell's free hand snapped out, catching the reptile behind the head.

It was a monstrously strong old critter and Kendell didn't figure it would have lived to such a ripe old age had it not been so. The tail thrashed and heaved upward, wrapping thick coils around his arm, twisting violently while its muscular body tried to tug its head back against his fingers. He clamped down on it until the snake stopped pulling back, but it didn't let up squeezing, lifting more heavy coils around his forearm.

He held the head well away from him, tightening up his grip, and turned his attention back to the Indians. They were all swinging back into their saddles when he looked back and the excitement in their voices was a language any man could understand. Even the old woman was cackling with glee now—suddenly they had a purpose and Kendell was pretty sure he knew what that purpose was—unfortunately, it was the same purpose as his own and he was of no mind to go and share his mission with anyone.

They rode south, toward the Dragoons, and after they

had dropped out of sight Kendell eased his way out of the grabbing mesquite with the writhing viper in his grasp.

Sidestepping nervously, the horse didn't like what Kendell carried from the bushes one bit, and he couldn't blame the animal. With his free hand he opened a pocket-knife and cut off the head, then stepped away from it. He knew enough about rattlesnakes to know that just because they're missing a head doesn't mean they still can't kill you. More than one thoughtless soul has met his maker through the nervous reflexes of a bodyless set of fangs. He took the body with him, holding it by the rattles, and even with its head gone it was still striking out. The critter just didn't know it was time to die.

He gutted it, wrapped it in a cloth and tucked it into his saddlebags—dinner tonight, he thought, recalling with some disdain the cold lump of jerky he'd been living off the last two days. He lifted the water bag to his lips and swished the warm water in his mouth, letting it surge down his dry throat.

In this Sonoran hell, water was worth more than gold, and as it moistened his lips it brought something else to mind. Remembering had become a bad habit, something he had not quite gotten under control yet. He capped the water bag and thought of the old church at San Pablo. Water had not been a scarce commodity in San Pablo. The well was deep and never dry; the cool water that gurgled from its rocky bowels—lifted by donkey pumps—splashed into a trough where the women came to wash clothes. The trough emptied out onto a lush garden, on the south side of the church, where it watered the ivy that climbed to the top of the bell tower and across the garden wall. In the spring lilacs bloomed and the girls of the village would come to spend the long, warm afternoons within the shade of the garden walls while their men worked the fields.

Not all the girls had men to call their own and give them children. María was one of those still looking for that right person to make her life complete. She may not have been the loveliest girl, but no one could have convinced Kendell of that—nor would it have made any difference. He recalled her face . . .

No! That was past. He shook loose of the thought and gazed up at the terrible sun burning down and the ugly birds swinging low overhead. The lonely buzzards somehow rescued him from his thoughts and the sun's glare burned his eyes—the pain of it was a lesser hurt than the ache which tore at his heart. He lowered his eyes again to the shimmering mountains ahead.

Something in the distance caught his eye and he squinted toward the east; the direction the small band of Indians had come from. A plume of black smoke was climbing off the desert floor, flattening out on its top and drifting away. It was perhaps five miles off and far too large to be just a campfire.

His jaw tightened and he looked back at the trail he had been following. Now there would be seven more horses on it and it would be an easy thing to locate again . . .

He studied the smoke once more, replaced the water bag and lifted himself painfully onto his horse. The wound in his side was on fire again, but he was getting pretty good at ignoring that particular pain. He turned east toward the smudge of smoke in the distance.

5

Cuchillo stopped his horse on a rise and scanned the vast, empty desert. Peering along the horizon, his dark eyes came once again to ponder the slight wisp of smoke curling off the desert floor.

Cochise was long dead and most of them who had followed him now lived on the reservation at San Carlos, but Cuchillo knew a few still remained free—the young ones, the angry ones who appeared suddenly, like the Wind Devil, without warning, to steal food, to kill, to strike out at the villages which lie to the south in the land called Mexico.

Cuchillo never quite understood the white man's division of the land—as if the Earth Mother were a thing which could be divided. The absurdity of it was beyond his grasp. This side they called the United States, that side Mexico. And to further confuse things, this place they named Arizona was not a state at all but something called a territory! . . . and it all made little difference to him. The desert was his home whether it stretched from one country to another. It was his home; he recognized no lines drawn on the white man's map.

Cuchillo studied the smoke and wondered what had brought them out of the mountains this time. The usual reasons, he knew; food, whiskey and ever-increasing boredom . . . and the hatred fired by what the white men had done to them. All valid reasons as far as he was concerned and he dismissed the thought, allowing a more troublesome notion to take its place.

His eyes turned back along the trail they had made coming down from the north. It was a barren track which few men would be able to follow for very long. Cuchillo shook his head. Sargot would have nothing to worry about for a while. Their pursuer was nowhere near now. He turned his horse back to camp aware of that tiny voice whispering inside of his head.

It was not a voice of words but of feelings and it was strong within the old Indian; Cuchillo knew better than to ignore such things.

As Cuchillo returned to camp he thought of the journey ahead of them. Two days' ride would bring them into the safety of the Dragoon Mountains . . . would bring Cuchillo home. Although it had been many years since he last made this trip, the trail leading to Cochise's old stronghold was a deeply trodden path in his mind. The stronghold had been a happy place for him, his family, his people; a hidden valley of only forty acres—as the white man measures land—with grass and water and game. And nearby were the secret burial grounds where his wife, his son, his friends and their great chief lay to this day.

It had been Cochise's funeral which had last brought Cuchillo to the place they were going to now. He recalled the procession through the little cave, the ceremony on the sacred place. Afterward they rested in the valley before returning to their land. Except for Cochise's close friend Tom Jeffords, no other white man was permitted to know of his final resting place; he alone was allowed to be present at the funeral.

Since that time Jeffords had moved on and had not returned. The Apaches—those who remain in the land—seldom venture into the stronghold. Stories around the campfires tell of Cochise's spirit moving through the valley.

Cuchillo would not deny the stories, but in life, Cochise and Cuchillo had been close friends. In death, the friendship would remain. If his spirit did indeed haunt the valley, it would understand.

What Sargot would do afterward, Cuchillo didn't know, but he did not trust the bearded man or his two companions. He did not trust men who killed women and children of their own people—who tortured the friendly, robed man who spoke to the God of the white men.

Cuchillo's misfortune was to have been locked up in the same jail cell with them. El Rito had been a one-horse, one-cell town. His only crime was to have Apache blood flowing through his veins. He never learned why Sargot and the others had been thrown into the same cell as he some hours later. The white men's affairs were their own business, and would have remained so had the night guard not strolled too close to the jail door. Without warning Sargot's huge hand darted through the bars and clamped a death grip around the startled man's throat. With his other hand, Sargot grabbed the ring of keys and a minute later they were all free.

At that time Cuchillo did not know them, and since he had no immediate plans himself, he agreed to lead them to a place of safety where they could wait before continuing on down into Mexico. The valley stronghold.

He thought he was doing it out of gratitude for being freed, but did not fully realize the true reason for wanting to return to that place now, just as he did not fully realize the true nature of Sargot and his friends. Not until they exposed the evil in their hearts at San Pablo. Now he knew them well—he'd known their kind before. And he knew something else, too. Gratitude played no part in his sudden desire to return to the stronghold.

If Cuchillo were a man to frown he would have now. Yet, it was of little value to show inner feelings to another, so his ancient face remained impassive as he came off the ridge and swung out of the saddle.

The sun had crept closer to the horizon, pushing the shadows beneath the ridge far out into the desert. Sargot looked up, watched Cuchillo lead his animal past the three women by the sandstone boulders and tie it to a mesquite there. He returned, squatted on his haunches by the three white men and shook his head.

"He is far away, to the east," he said, lifting an arm in the direction.

"How do you know that?"

Cuchillo shrugged his shoulders. "I know. There is smoke; the Apaches have come out of the mountains again. He will follow the smoke. He is far away now, but he will come."

"Apaches! That's a fine pot of beans. We not only have someone trailing us, but now you tell me there's a war party in the area, too."

Cuchillo shook his head. "No war party. Cochise is dead. Geronimo is on the reservation. No more leaders; no more wars. Just some Indians maybe drink too much whiskey."

"Well I don't like it," Sargot snapped angrily.

"I do not like it, too," Cuchillo agreed. "That is why we must travel at night now. It will be safer."

Jake Sargot grunted.

Ben Jones said, "Hell, what are we running for? Let's just wait here and jump that fellow when he comes by. That wouldn't be no problem at all."

Sargot considered this, looking at the Indian, but Cuchillo shook his head.

"Why the hell not?" Jones demanded.

"We not have enough water. We wait two, maybe three days for this man to come upon us, then we ride two more days before we reach water? No, no good, anyway, this man who follows our trail through this desert is too clever to allow himself to be caught in a trap—he is no ordinary man; he is with a demon . . ."

"Demon? He ain't no more than flesh and blood and that means he can be killed."

Cuchillo shrugged his shoulders at the skinny man's words and looked down to the dust beneath his moccasins. In a moment the tip of his finger began to draw a symbol in the sand.

"Well?" Jones demanded of him but Cuchillo appeared not to hear. "Well, Jake?" He looked back at Sargot.

"The Indian is right," Sargot said, "we can't afford to wait around in this damn hell until he shows up."

"You ain't gonna listen to that crazy old Indian, are you, Jake?"

Sargot laughed. "I don't listen to nobody what ain't talking sense and right now he's talking sense. You ain't. Tell you what, Jones, since you're so all fired up to waylay that tracker, why don't you stay behind, catch up with us later if you think you can?"

Ben Jones grinned and shook his head. "No thanks, 'fraid that ain't the way it works, Jake. You see, I got me a stake in what's on the back of that mule and in at least one of them women, too. Nope, you ain't getting shed of me that easily. I'm gonna stick by you and Pedro like a cocklebur on a hounddog's back until we reach Mexico and split it all up."

"Have it your way, Jones, but if you stay it's with the clear understanding that I give the orders and you take them, because if you don't"—and Sargot's mouth twisted in an evil grin—"if you don't, well Pedro and me, we just might be splitting up an extra share of that church gold when we cross the border."

Pedro glanced up, saying, "Sounds like a good deal to me, Jake."

Jones glared at the Mexican, then back into the bearded man's hard brown eyes. They were eyes that sent needles up his spine, the eyes of a man who meant every word he spoke. Jones forced a grin to his face. "All right, Jake, you're boss," he said, and moved away from him. Sargot's eyes never softened as they followed him.

Cuchillo seemed unaware of the confrontation as he completed the symbol in the sand, removed his medicine bag from around his neck and placed it in the center of it. Rocking slowly on his haunches, he started a low chant. Sargot blinked and looked back at Cuchillo, then stood and left the old Indian alone.

"Where are you taking us?" Olinda Flores demanded of Sargot when he stood over them.

"None of your concern," he told her, turning an eye on Juana Gutiérrez. "You're mine. I picked you. You can make it easy on yourself or you can make it hard and I don't much care."

Sargot hovered over Juana a moment, waiting for her reply. Juana averted her eyes, staring vacantly at the ground and when she finally lifted them to view Sargot's face they were filled with tears. Even so, they were pretty eyes, dark and mysterious, and the people of San Pablo used to say to her father, "Onesimo, she has your eyes, and Rosina's full lips."

Onesimo would laugh proudly and answer, *"Sí,* and every day I thank the Lord above that he did not give to my Juana this beak of a nose too or these big cow ears, heh?"

As a child, Juana found pleasure and security in that deep, hearty laugh—now it all seemed so very far away. In this place, with Sargot, nothing of pleasure could ever be found.

Juana bit back her tears. "Why?" she asked.

"Because I say so and you don't need to know any more reason." He untied her from her friends while the other two girls looked on with horror. Juana's fate was their fate also and they knew there was no one left who could rescue them from it.

Sargot pulled the girl to her feet by her thin wrists and she struggled against his powerful grip as he led her across the sand and behind a mesquite hummock. Violently, she resisted, but it did little good to struggle against such a bear of a man. In the end, Juana was helpless but to obey his whims.

6

Kendell reined in and studied the small valley below where a stream trickled softly. It probably had its headwaters somewhere up in the Dragoons, which were still far to the west. The stream fed a stand of tall cottonwood trees and a thick tangle of scrub oak before twisting out of a tight canyon and across a wide valley where the land opened up, tall with stiff brown grass. A line of trees stretched out into the valley too, following the sparkling ribbon as it flowed away.

It was what some people would call pastoral, Kendell mused; a pleasant and welcome sight to a man accustomed to the burning sand and prickly cactus . . . The fact that the cabin alongside the stream was ablaze, that three arrows protruded from the slick, black coat of a dog sprawled in agonizing death in an empty corral, that two bloodied bodies lay atop each other on the ground in front of the smoking cabin, however, did much to detract from the pleasant-little-valley image and only tended to rekindle the bitterness which was already consuming his soul.

Kendell frowned as he studied the gutted cabin sitting quietly in the valley—so that was what they had been up to. They had stolen the horses and run off whatever cattle had been nearby; cattle don't travel well in the desert without water. They killed whatever moved and left them to the buzzards. Well, God has a way of cleaning up the messes His unruly creations leave behind and here the buzzards were that way. Creations! he scoffed. If God *had* created man in his image, Kendell wasn't so sure he'd ever want to meet up with this Almighty Creator!

He turned his horse away from the valley; it was none of his business anyway. His business lay ahead, in the Dragoon Mountains, and he figured a course set due west into the setting sun would bring him across their tracks. Only now there was a complication; he'd have to ride drag on a pack of renegades—well, that was preferable to continually watching his backside. He started his animal toward the mountains.

In the waning light of evening, shadows were already moving down from the distant peaks, filling the valleys and softening the stark outline of the mountains ahead. Their western slope glowed a rosy, almost bloody tinge. He recalled that in the days of Cochise the Dragoons had been a stronghold of sorts for the famous Apache chief, and as he thought of the bodies down by the cabin he wondered if the renegades who had done that had once rode with Cochise. At that thought he stopped and looked back at the cabin; a fold of rock hid it from view but a trail of gray smoke rising high into the still air marked its location.

He was this close; he might just as well go on back and bury them . . . No! That was his old self speaking, he countered, frowning again. It was going to take a while to finally bury that old self, too, that old way of thinking, for it was as dead as those two bodies down by the cabin. Well, it was almost dark and he'd be stopping anyway. At least here was fresh water and grass for his animal; he didn't figure the Apaches would be coming back anytime soon either. All in all, returning had its benefits, he told himself, reining his horse around. All right, so the old self won this one—he'd fare better the next time.

The place looked deserted but as a precaution he loosened the hammer thong on his pistol and drew the Winchester from its scabbard before starting down the steep trail.

It was quiet . . . and the heaviness of death hung in the still air. The birds, if any were near, were silent. He approached the cabin, aware of only the even plod of his horse and the brittle crackling of burning wood inside the building. Wood smoke choked the air as he drew closer. Behind the house stood a privy with its door limping open on one hinge. To the north, along the stream and bordering the cottonwoods was a string of corrals, empty but for the dog. A two-stall barn and a tack house stood next to the corrals —both appeared untouched.

Kendell halted his horse in front of the cabin above the bodies of the man and woman. She was naked and her body had been thrown on top of her man, or perhaps that had been only as far as she managed to crawl before dying. Kendell couldn't be sure. An arrow in her back had produced very little blood and it appeared she had already been dead. Her hair was gone and the man had not had enough hair to make it worth their while. From his looks he had been a good ten to fifteen years older than the woman.

Kendell dismounted, aware of a cool uneasiness running up his spine; his side ached but he ignored it for the moment, bending over her. She had been a young woman and she might have been pretty too but that was hard to determine now. He turned her over—

His brain exploded. Staggering back, he clutched his reeling head while his eyes fixed wide upon her body. The savages had taken a knife to her, had cut out her breasts, leaving two bloodied gashes in her chest. Kendell's stomach wrenched and he turned away, fighting back the memories . . . but they came just the same.

Suddenly the church was burning around him and he was back in the middle of those raging flames. María was in his arms and the choking smoke clutched at their throats and stung their eyes, but somehow they managed to make it outside.

Coughing, they stumbled out into the street where gunfire and the cries of panic-stricken people made a confusing sound. The smoke had blinded him and his lungs burned, but María was safe . . .

Then a shot rang out nearby and the nightmare took a nasty twist. María fell from his arms and something warm flowed onto his hands. It was a long, agonizing moment before his eyes cleared and then he saw María lying in the street by the well. He started for her when a rider came around the corner of the church swinging a rifle. He had appeared suddenly and Kendell would never forget that long, skinny face—like the rest of the man's body—he'd take that memory to the grave. The rifle barrel swung out, striking him across the face; his feet went out from under him and the world turned black—and black it has stayed. In another minute his eyes opened. He raised his head from the dusty street and by the well he saw the knife flash in the skinny man's hand—then he saw María and her bloodied blouse ripped open . . .

Kendell dragged himself to his feet too weak to do any good, but he tried. With a single thrust the knife buried deep into his side and that was all he could remember—but that face, he would never forget it while he had breath in his body . . . long, beardless, evil . . .

The memory left him as suddenly and swiftly as it had overcome him and Kendell found himself hanging limp onto the saddle, uncontrollable tears streaming off his cheeks. He straightened, wiping his eyes and looking back at the mangled body upon the ground. Damn her, he whispered under his breath. This time had been worse than the last.

He rolled her back onto her husband, aware of a certain cool detachment now. The feeling of compassion that should have been there was not to be found in Kendell's heart. That feeling had died with María. Burying them was an unpleasant task that had to be done and he went about it in a steely, mechanical manner.

He found a shovel in the tack house and the soft ground behind the cabin yielded easily; by the time the sun had dropped below the ragged western horizon Kendell had covered them both and was carefully patting the top of the mound into a smooth hump with the back of the shovel. He put the both of them in one hole—somehow he felt that was the way they would have wanted it. He finished smoothing down the mound, and stood back, knowing he could have done better for them but his heart wasn't in it. Words should have been spoken over them; however, Kendell could not abide the hypocrisy of such a deed, so he just stood there looking down at the grave for a long time. Darkness had settled in when he returned to the horse and untied his saddlebags.

Kendell put together a small fire out behind the tack house, down by the stream where the smoldering house was out of sight, and unwrapped the rattlesnake. He had his lump of jerked beef and coffee but it was already old fare; the rattlesnake would be a pleasant change. Snake meat wasn't half bad if you cooked it proper and weren't squeamish in the stomach. It was a light, white meat and it always reminded him of fish—maybe it was all those bones that made him think of fish. He skinned the fat reptile and sliced it up for roasting, then he hung a pot of water over the fire, and while it was working up to a boil, he started along the stream to scrounge dry wood.

The sky was clear with a crescent moon hanging like a slice of melon on the edge of the valley. By the time he returned with his arms full of wood the moon had climbed higher into the sky and lost its orange tint. It was a bright sliver now, casting a pale glow upon the broad valley. In the dark, the smoldering cabin came alive with the red flickering of burning embers, and now with the cold moonlight shining overhead he could see the little kangaroo rats hopping about on the barren ground which separated him from the cabin.

As he returned to his campfire the creaking of a board startled him; the firewood fell from his arms as his gun came from its holster in such an easy, fluid movement that it surprised him. He'd been good with a gun once, shortly after the war when he had worked his way west to California, to try his hand at the gold fields. The journey had left behind a string of young, raw towns where the only safe ticket of passage was a fast gun and hard fists, and Kendell had had both, but that was a long time ago with a lot of fallow time between.

The creaking stopped and Kendell remained motionless,

listening as a faint scraping noise reached his ears. It was the sound of someone crawling, and the Apaches came to mind as he stepped away from the glow of the fire and backed up against the rough-hewed log siding of the tack house. Half stumbling in the dark over a stack of lumber piled there, he inched to the front of the building and his eyes swung across the pale, moonlit grounds. Aside from the rats, nothing else moved. Kendell kicked open the wooden door and the stillness within the little tack house was complete. The shadows there concealed no secret enemy as he stepped inside with his gun cocked and his finger on the trigger. In the darkness of the place, he stood listening a moment. The scuffing returned, then something brushed the boards beneath his boots.

It could have been an animal; maybe a skunk or one hell of a big rat, but Kendell didn't think so. Animals generally moved more carefully than that. Whatever was under the building was not used to cramped quarters and now was trying to rearrange its position. Perhaps it was only a fat, clumsy skunk . . . perhaps . . . but he wasn't in any mood to take chances and he pointed the barrel of his pistol at the floorboards touching the trigger. Then he remembered the pile of boards he'd nearly tripped over alongside the building and released a long breath, uncocking the pistol as he moved back outside.

Something had nagged at him when he first rode up to the place earlier that evening and now he knew what it was. He studied the lumber in the dark; in the old days a setup like this was common practice with settlers in Indian territory. He'd run across it a time or two on his way to California, but that was back when Indian trouble was a way of life; today in 1898 there weren't supposed to be Indian raids —he guessed the ones that did this destruction hadn't heard yet. He started to work at the pile and when he'd thrown aside the last board he stepped away from the hole and said, "Whoever you are underneath there, come on out while you're still able."

In a moment a round, pink face poked out; smudged and grimy and with eyes wide as twenty-dollar gold pieces. She blinked up at Kendell. A little voice said, "Please, mister, don't shoot me . . ."

"Come on out of there." He pushed the gun back into the holster.

She squirmed out from under the building and he helped her to her feet. After wiping her hands on the dirty dress, she looked back up at him and there was fear in her eyes which she tried hard not to show. He figured she couldn't have been any more than ten at the most. She shifted on her feet and said, "Are you going to hurt us, mister?"

"Us?" Kendell glanced back at the hole and the girl stiffened. "Who else is down there?"

She shook her head quickly and her eyes grew even larger. "Ain't no one else down there, mister, it was just me, that's all," she said, biting down on her lower lip, watching him intently with round eyes.

Kendell grimaced. "I wouldn't ever take up poker, little lady," he said, moving her to the side. "Come on out of there; I'm not going to hurt you . . . come on."

Another small, pink face. He gave the little boy a hand up, standing him next to his sister. He was six inches shorter, dressed in grubby overalls equally as filthy as his sister's blue gingham dress. Looking at the dress brought a sudden ache to Kendell's heart as he recalled where he had seen its match. It didn't take a trained eye to see it had been a mother and daughter set, and it didn't take any effort at all to imagine the love and time that went into the making of them. The hours of enjoyment it must have brought the both of them, he thought; it seemed a sin the dress should now decorate that crazy old hag's back. Well, so what, he countered, it was none of his affair. Still, the notion tugged at his heart, and that was impossible since his heart was already dead and buried.

He decided they must have been under there most of the day; they were surely scared and hungry and grief-filled over their parents' death—and then it occurred to him that these two did not yet know the extent of their loss. They could not have piled those boards over the hole once inside, that had to be done for them, by parents who loved them, not renegades out for blood.

It was none of his affair, he reminded himself again. He'd done the proper thing by burying them, so what more could the children expect of him. The world was full of problems and he couldn't be expected to solve them all—it was best now that he'd finally stop trying.

"How long have you two been under there?"

The girl's small shoulders made a shrug. "I don't rightly know . . . all day, I reckon. Mommy put Willie and me into the hideaway this morning when they saw the Indians come off the ridge." She pointed at the moonlit skyline. "They were up there."

The little boy turned his eyes to Kendell. "Where is my mommy?"

He grimaced. The girl was watching him, too. "What's your name?" he asked her.

"Jemima," she said.

"Jemima," he repeated, "and Willie," glancing at the lad.

The girl nodded.

"You got a last name to go along with the first?"

"Butler."

"Jemima Butler and Willie Butler," he said, looking at the two children. "Well, Jemima Butler and Willie Butler, I've a fire burning in back; it'll keep you warm, and you're welcome to my coffee and my food, which there isn't much of, but there's enough."

Willie moved away from his sister's side, stood at the corner of the tack house and gazed at the smoldering remains of his home.

Kendell went to the boy, turning him around by the shoulders. Willie's eyes were wide and watery and a tear ran a muddy streak down his cheek.

"Where's my mommy and daddy?" he demanded, blinking at Kendell.

He'd sidestepped that question once and it had come back at him, now it would be a burden to keep the truth from them, and it wasn't quite fair either. A twinge of an old feeling rose to the surface and he quickly suppressed it, allowing bitterness to take its place while recalling the unwanted memories that seeing the children's mother had brought on. Well, the kid had asked twice now and he had a right to know the truth.

"Your mother is dead, and so is your father. I buried them behind the house." They were hard words for a child to hear and he didn't try to temper them. Tears filled Willie's little eyes and Jemima put an arm around his shoulders. Kendell left the children alone with their grief and went back to gather up the firewood he had dropped.

The water was hot and he fixed himself coffee. On the end of long, thin twigs he had skewered cubes of rattlesnake meat and had hung them over the coals. He gave each stick a turn now and brought the coffee cup to his lips, aware of the children coming up silently behind him.

"Come on in and have a sit," he said without looking back at them. "You drink coffee, Jemima?"

She nodded her head. "Sometimes Mommy lets me have a cup of coffee; she puts lots of milk in it."

"Well, don't have any milk here," he replied, looking at Willie's tearstained face. He dug into his saddlebags for two more cups, filled one with coffee and the other with water.

"I reckon you're still a mite too young to be drinking coffee," he said, handing Willie the water. They sat down on the grass and clutched their cups while Kendell tended the meat on the fire.

They handled their grief well; Kendell wished he could do the same. Watching them, he recalled a verse from the Bible he had read. *Suffer the little children to come unto me, and forbid them not: for of such is the kingdom of God*—or so it went. Thinking back on it now, Kendell decided that it was just as well that it was meant for the kids, for he wanted no part in it.

The snake looked cooked; he took it from the coals, offering some to the children.

"What is it?" Jemima wanted to know, turning the stick with the cube of meat on it over, examining it suspiciously.

"Rattlesnake." He took a bite of it.

"Rattlesnake?" Her nose twisted and she handed the stick back to Kendell. "I . . . I don't think I want to eat it. Thank you just the same."

Willie wasn't sure either and Kendell figured the boy would have eaten it all right if it wasn't that now he was looking to Jemima for leadership.

"I reckon you just aren't hungry, then," Kendell grunted.

"I'm starving," Willie said quickly.

"Hush!"

He glanced at his sister. "But I am."

Kendell stuck the meat back over the coals and removed a cloth-wrapped lump from his saddlebags.

"What is that?" she asked him.

"Jerked beef. I reckon this will be more to your liking."

Jemima nodded her head while Willie's pink tongue slid quickly across his lip. Kendell sliced a ribbon of jerky for each of them and the rattlesnake was all his. He made short work of it.

Afterward they sat around the fire but no one was really in any mood for conversation. They each had private thoughts needing attention, personal wounds which had to be licked and cared for. The night was alive with sounds; the clicking of crickets, the croaking of spadefoot toads—it made a soothing music for the three doleful people and in a short time the children were asleep in each other's arms. Kendell pulled a blanket over them, settling back to listen to the night sounds, but he didn't hear any beauty in them.

In the loneliness of the night his mind flashed back and forth over the course of his life; the campfire and the clear starry sky reminded him of the long trek west to California in the days of his youth, after the war. It reminded him of the lonely towns and the lonely people along the trail from Virginia to that far western state. He recalled the long periods of introspection along the way, muddled and confused by the urgent need to survive. A need which taught him how to use a six-shooter and use it well. Finally he recalled the day when his life came to that fork in the road. He'd taken the road he thought right, and he'd been a fool . . .

Slowly the night and his past slipped away; the soothing night sounds and cool air worked on his tired spirit. The fire burned low, his eyes became heavy. A distant coyote arguing with the moon was too much for Kendell to resist. Its lonely call was a song of despair; a tune matching perfectly the beat of his consciousness and the march of his soul.

7

Matt Kendell blinked awake suddenly. The eastern sky was gray with the dawn. For a moment he laid there not moving; listening and remembering. His mind ran through the previous day's events; the exhausting ride across the desert, the renegades and that strange woman, the burned-out cabin, the two orphaned children . . . He discovered he was frowning. Other thoughts would come if he wasn't careful. The crickets and toads were still chirping merrily away and their sound was reassuring. If he had awoken to silence it would have meant they were not alone.

Sitting up, he looked at the children curled into each other, sleeping peacefully beneath the blanket. The fire was cold and he put on some sticks, rekindling a blaze; in a few minutes a new fire crackled and he stood, rubbing his arms to get the blood moving. A fresh scab had formed over the wound in his side and the skin stretched painfully as he got to his feet. It cut like a sharp razor and he winced, then he walked down into the cottonwood trees behind the corrals.

When he returned the sky was brighter, but here in the valley shadows still clung to the ground. That's the nature of valleys, he knew; first place to see the dusk and the last to get the morning light. It puzzled him why anyone would choose to live in a place such as that and he pondered that a moment while quietly filling the coffeepot and hanging it over the fire. Well, the land looked promising and Kendell decided a farmer would most likely be taking other things into consideration, such as good water, protection from the wind and plentiful grass to feed his stock. He had plied many trades in his younger days, but sodbusting had never been one of them.

Jemima stirred then continued breathing slow and rhythmically. The smell of smoldering wood hung heavy in the air and a few red embers still glowed in the chinks of the cabin, but for the most part the building was no more than a pile of coarse ash.

Kendell finished his coffee, packed his gear and was saddling his horse by the time the sun broke over the rim of the valley; a bright yellow orb that would dog him like a branding iron the rest of the day. He regretted having to leave the coolness of the valley, but the heat of the desert was like ice water compared to the fire of revenge that consumed his heart.

Jemima Butler came awake with the sun and sat up rubbing her eyes, looking for Kendell. Quietly she left her brother's side and came to him as he was tightening the cinches. When he slipped his saddle carbine into its scabbard the question was in her eyes—blue eyes, Kendell noted, seeing them for the first time by the light of day. The question was plain on her young face but he chose to ignore it. It was his right! She was old enough to look after herself, he told himself, swinging up onto his saddle and turning the horse away from the homestead.

"Mister—?" Jemima said timidly.

He halted his horse.

"Mister?"

Kendell looked back reluctantly. Her large eyes watched

him closely. She had washed her face in the stream the night before and tugged a comb through the tangles of her long yellow hair, but her dress was still grimy, and despite the ten-year-old's valiant efforts, she still looked like a homeless waif. Well, he reminded himself, that was, after all, what she now was.

"Mister, are you going to leave us here?" she asked.

Kendell grimaced, looking straight ahead. "I can't take you where I'm going," he told her. He had his own problems and they had theirs. Kendell gave a flick on the reins and started away from the homestead.

"Mister?" she said. "What should I do? Where should I take my little brother?"

Kendell stopped his horse again but he didn't look back. He wanted to tell her to go to the church at San Pablo, that the priest there would take care of her, but there was no priest at San Pablo anymore and the church was gone. There was no place for her and her brother in San Pablo now, even if, alone, she *were* able to cross the burning desert on foot and without water.

He looked up at the peaks of the Dragoon Mountains shining in the sunlight. That's where they were heading, he told himself, and he was pretty sure he knew where up in those mountains they were aiming for, recalling the old Apache who had accompanied them. But the place was a secret and he'd have to be a sharp tracker to locate it, or find someone who was, if he ever was going to catch up with them. It suddenly became imperative for him to find them before they made it to their destination. Another reason he couldn't be burdened with the children.

He looked back at the burned-out hulk of Jemima's

home. From where he sat, astride his horse, he could see the mound behind the house. The freshly overturned earth was already dry. In a month the weeds would have grown a blanket over the grave and by next spring they'd have full run of the whole homestead. In a few years a man would have to look closely to find the spot where Jemima and Willie's house had stood, where their parents had spilled out their life, where the earth had covered them.

Kendell looked at Jemima; a wisp of a girl not yet a woman and not quite a child anymore. Willie was still asleep by the fire, unaware that already this little girl had assumed full responsibility for his welfare—a job at times greater than some adults were able to manage. They would make out all right, he tried to tell himself, but the truth was not so easily shed. Their food was gone and so was their home; a child can live just so long on water and dandelion leaves before starvation and pneumonia would snuff them out—that is if the Apaches didn't return first . . .

But where could two children fit into his plan . . . his mission? They'd end up dead if he took them along and they would surely die if he left them.

Well, he had his own worries; he didn't need theirs too. He had stopped trying to save the world, he reminded himself bitterly, and that included Jemima and Willie Butler. He turned away, kicking his horse into motion. Following the stream up the valley, he did not look back—he couldn't bring himself to see Jemima's eyes as she watched her only hope riding away. At the ridge he stopped. The Dragoons already stood indistinct through the shimmering morning heat. He chanced a glance over his shoulder; the cabin was but a gray pile of ash at this distance and thankfully he could not see Jemima.

He nudged his horse ahead with his eyes fixed on the glaring white sand, but it didn't seem to be working now. The last few days he had been able to use the burning desert as a substitute for the pain in his heart, but this time the new ache there was too much to mask. Glancing across the desert to the Dragoons, Jemima's blue eyes haunted him. It was no good. He cursed himself and yanked the horse's head around.

She was still standing there where he had left her; staring at the smoldering heap . . . and crying. He stopped his horse and she spun around startled, then wiped her eyes with the sleeve of her dress. She'd not let him see her crying!

He spent a long time studying the child in the morning light, wishing he had never nosied in—but he had, and he drew a deep breath snorting it back out. "Well, go wake up your brother and make it quick if you want to come along. We are going to have to carry more water; I saw a canteen hanging inside the tack house. Does it still hold water?"

Jemima's eyes brightened. "Yes, sir, Mister Kendell—no, it don't leak nowhere," and she ran back to Willie, shaking him awake.

"Wake up, Willie," she said, "wake up, we're leaving!"

Willie stirred, rubbing his eyes, and she left him, hurrying into the tack house, reappearing a moment later carrying the canteen in one hand and dragging an old, brass-framed Henry repeating rifle with the other.

Kendell climbed off his horse and took the rifle from her, checking for a loaded chamber. "Where in the Devil . . . ?" he had started to say.

"It was my pa's," she said; "he had it hidden in case we ever needed it. It's fully loaded; he kept it that way. Pa always said an empty gun ain't no gun at all." She paused as her eyes fell upon the bloodied shirt.

"You've been hurt," she said suddenly, seeing the crusty bloodstain for the first time.

He looked down at himself, a little surprised at the horror in her eyes. He had just sort of gotten used to the great crusty stain and the occasional fresh spots of blood which would dampen it—he hadn't really seen it for what it was.

"It's going to be all right," he told her.

"Maybe I should look at it—"

"No." He retreated from her hands.

She frowned at him. "The least we can do is wash it. You don't want to get an infection, do you?"

It had never occurred to him to tend to it; perhaps, deep down inside, he didn't really care one way or the other.

"Well?" She looked up at him, waiting for an answer. "You can wash it in the stream. The water is good; ain't never had no problem with it."

"We don't have time for that," he told her.

"And once we get into the desert we won't have the water," she replied in a reprimanding voice, and Kendell saw in her a striking image of what the little girl's mother must have been like. Strong-willed and protective of what was hers—suddenly Jemima had adopted him and she'd be hanged if she wasn't going to look out for his well-being despite his objections.

Kendell drew in another breath but there was no arguing with this new guardian of his, especially since she was absolutely right. "All right," he conceded, "I'll go and splash some water on it—by myself. You get yourself and Willie ready to ride." He took the canteen from her hand and started down to the stream.

"There's a bar of lye soap on a stump down there and a towel, too," she called after him.

"Yes, ma'am," he said over his shoulder.

When he returned Jemima and Willie were behind the cabin and a frown soured his face as he went to them. Jemima looked up, wiping away a tear; she had some blue cloth clutched in her arms. Kendell put a hand on her shoulder.

"Say your good-byes," he said. "They will always be with you—in here," and he touched his heart. He didn't know what had made him say that.

Jemima forced a smile to her face but it was too much to hold back and she buried her head on Kendell's side, sobbing bitterly. Willie cried too. He put a hand on the boy's shoulder, allowing them a moment to get the tears out. Finally Jemima sniffed and pushed herself away from him. "Here, this is for you," she said, handing him the blue bundle. "It was Pa's. It's clean. It had been on the clothesline and I found it over there in the weeds."

Kendell unfolded the shirt and grimaced. "Thanks," he said. "I reckon I can use it."

"The one you're wearing looks horrible," she said with a frown, but her voice was firming up. She was a real trouper, he thought, pulling off his shirt.

Jemima's eyes went wide. He had told her it was nothing, but the ugly scab running up his side called him a liar. She turned her eyes away and he pulled her father's shirt on, leaving the top corner of the bib unbuttoned.

"We better be leaving," he said, tucking the shirttail into his pants.

Jemima took Willie's hand and followed Kendell to the horse. He tied the Henry rifle in place, slinging the canteen over the saddle horn, then mounted up, hoisting Willie onto the saddle in front of him. Jemima climbed up behind the cantle atop his bedroll and wrapped her arms around his waist.

He turned the horse away and left the homestead behind.

8

"Why are we stopping?"

Kendell ignored the girl's question. "Slide off the back," he said.

She slipped to the ground so that he could swing his leg stiffly around and dismount. He stooped to examine the tracks in the sand. It had taken less time than he had reckoned, cutting due west, to cross the trail he had been following the previous day. The tracks told him the Indians had already passed here; they were ahead of him and he didn't have to watch his back. But now the sand was firming up, forming hard, flat stretches in places—desert pavement was the word that came to mind. He'd encountered the substance before and where it occurred now the trail became indistinct. It brought a scowl to his face.

"What is it—what's wrong?" Jemima asked him again.

"Apaches," Kendell replied, climbing back onto his horse, giving her a hand up. "The same bunch that murdered your ma and pa."

"Are you going to follow them, Mister Kendell?" she asked.

"Uh-huh."

"Isn't that dangerous?"

"Yes, ma'am."

"What about my little brother? I don't want him getting hurt."

"Willie hasn't got any say-so in the matter and neither do you. Just consider yourself lucky I'm taking you and your brother along at all and don't get pushy. You can be dropped off anywhere."

Jemima didn't reply to this but Kendell was aware of her small arms loosening up a mite around his waist. Willie remained silent as he had been most of the trip, uttering hardly a word since leaving the homestead. He appeared unaware of what was going on around him, spending his time staring off at the glaring desert floor, occasionally wiping his eyes with the sleeve of his shirt. Perhaps, Kendell wondered, the boy was using his old trick for easing the pain he felt inside.

He dismissed the kids from mind and that was a mistake; it made room for the memories to flood in. The desert seemed to fade around him and he once again heard María's laughing voice and saw her smiling face before him like a taunting ghost.

Taunting. It was an appropriate word, he decided. Even in death she taunted him, for now, as it was when she had been alive, he could not have her. He recalled her small, dark face, her burning black eyes alive with a passion for life —a passion he could only share from afar. Look, don't touch, that was the rule, wasn't it? Damn the rules! At times it nearly drove him crazy, but he had made his choice and although at times he hated it, it was done, made; too late for one Matt Kendell.

Slowly his thoughts came around to the men who had ridden into San Pablo late that Saturday evening. They were an odd group. He had watched them ride down from the north and tie up in front of the cantina; two whites, a Mexican and an Apache. They dismounted and talked a moment on the boardwalk outside, then three of them went into the cantina while the Apache stayed outside. Shortly afterward he strolled over to the well by the church for a drink. Kendell recalled the Indian's broken-tooth smile when he walked over to speak with him. He had a feeling it was a smile that rarely showed on the old man's face.

"The water is good after so many miles of desert," he had said, looking up from the bucket at Kendell.

"Where are you and your friends bound for?" he had asked him.

The Indian shrugged his shoulders. "I do not know the thoughts of the white men," he answered. "They ask me to lead them many places. They say they want to come to San Pablo, to visit the famous church." His black eyes glanced up at the steeple. "The church of the white man's God is very big."

"The white man has a very big God," he had replied, smiling.

The Indian nodded his head. "It must be so; I have seen his house in many parts of the land where my people once spoke with our gods."

"You and your friends intend to stay?"

He shook his head. "They are not my friends. I lead them through the desert, that is all. They want to go into Mexico, to Janos. They want me to lead. Janos!" The Indian stared into Kendell's eyes. "It is a bad place, Janos is. Geronimo's woman was murdered in Janos. Geronimo never forgive Janos for that; it is well he is living on the government reservation or there would be much blood on the land."

The Indian left to tend the horses while the three wayfarers who had come to San Pablo, Kendell observed wryly, to *visit the famous church* appeared, at the moment, more interested in visiting the cantina and the girls there.

He recalled the lights burning long into the night and the raucous, drunken sounds coming from the cantina. The drinking continued throughout the night and in early morning he was awakened by the crash of breaking window glass. When he peered through his curtains, flames were already licking out of the cantina's windows. The three men stood in the street; whiskey bottles and guns in hand . . . The Apache was not among them.

He remembered dressing hurriedly and rushing out into the street, but it was already too late to stop what had started.

Neither Jemima nor Willie interrupted his brooding and he rode along unaware of the blistering heat, or the trail he was following, or that the sun was dropping low and the air starting to cool. His subconscious was still alert, but consciously, he could have continued on oblivious to the world around him had his stomach not cried out for food. Reining in, he realized the day was gone and the sun would soon be down.

A cluster of brown sandstone rocks looked like a good place to stop and he turned his horse toward them. He lowered Willie to the ground while Jemima slid off the horse's rump. She took her brother's hand, standing out of the way to watch Kendell unsaddle the horse and tie the animal near a patch of brown grass.

Willie fidgeted impatiently at his sister's side. "I'm hungry," he whispered.

Jemima gave him a nudge. "Hush!"

Kendell opened his saddlebags and removed the old lump of jerky, viewing it narrowly. He looked at Willie shuffling his feet, eyeing that hard lump in the same regretful way.

"I know what you mean, son," he said. He gave the problem some consideration. "How about we get us some real meat?" A hunting trip is just what the kid needed to get his mind off his problems—it wouldn't do him any harm, either.

"There must be a thousand big old jackrabbits out there just begging to fill our bellies." Kendell watched the boy's eyes brighten. He removed his rifle from its scabbard then eyed the old Henry repeater that had belonged to Willie's father. It was a time-worn piece which had seen much use; a rimfire .44 with a brass receiver that was tarnished. All the original sharp edges were worn smooth and round. The stock was gouged and cracked and the barrel had lost its blueing and rust pitted the inside of the bore. There was a deep nick in the magazine tube but the gun still functioned flawlessly and Kendell reckoned, if nothing else, it was just the ticket they needed for hunting jackrabbits.

"How old are you, Willie?"

The boy hesitated. "Eight years old, mister," he said.

"Eight?" Kendell made a face. "Well then, I reckon you're nearly full grown. Your pa ever teach you to shoot?"

He shook his head. "No, sir."

"Well, I reckon he was getting ready to then." Kendell handed the Henry rifle to the boy. "You see that lever on the bottom? That loads the rounds into the chamber and cocks the hammer at the same time." He demonstrated.

"Shucks, Mister Kendell," Willie said frowning, "I know

that already; even Jemima knows that. We've watched Pa do it a hundred times."

"Even Jemima?" Kendell raised an eyebrow. "You see, your pa did teach you something about shooting."

"Pa never let me shoot the gun but I watched him plenty of times."

"Then you've got the hardest part licked. All that is left to show you is how to aim it—he ever show you that?"

"No."

"Well, this is how you go about it. First you snuggle the rifle into your shoulder like this." He helped Willie get the long gun into position. It was a bit lengthy for the boy's arms but nothing which couldn't be overcome with a little effort and some stretching. He explained the principle of sighting along the front and rear sights and when Willie appeared to have the hang of it Kendell said, "I'm getting mighty hungry and that old sun is going down; I'd say it's just about the right time for those jacks to be poking their long-eared heads out of their burrows, so let's see what kind of luck we have."

He started out into the desert with Jemima at his side and Willie—his arms wrapped round that long rifle—struggling with the weapon to keep it from getting hung up in the sage and mesquite. Kendell watched him, amused, and recalled another boy who had had similar problems—only instead of the deserts of Arizona it was in the mountains of Virginia, and the rifle was a long, single-shot percussion squirrel gun. It was a warm memory that brought a smile to his lips as he saw his father's proud face when he had bagged that first gray squirrel . . .

He became aware of the smile and let the memory fade. He had no right smiling now. He remembered San Pablo.

Without warning a jackrabbit broke from a clump of snakeweed and darted out into the open. It stopped suddenly after a dozen feet as if frozen, its long ears straight up in the air.

"Remember what I showed you?" Kendell whispered.

"Uh-huh." Willie put the rifle to his shoulder and struggled to get his finger on the trigger. Kendell thumbed the hammer back for him and the long barrel wobbled as the boy yanked back on the trigger. The bullet kicked up a spit of sand two feet short and the rabbit took off. Kendell threw his own rifle to his shoulder, bringing the fleeing hare in line and firing. It tumbled across the sand and stopped.

Jemima and Willie hurried ahead to collect the game while Kendell followed after them, shaking his head in mild amazement. It had been years since he had marked a moving target with a snap shot like that—back when he had been in tune with a gun. All those years seemed not to matter now; he was perhaps a bit slower and lacked the fine tuning he once had, but he was still good, and with a little practice all that old polish would return. Some things a man just never forgets, he mused.

"Gee, Mister Kendell, that's some shootin'! Can you teach me to shoot like that?" Willie's voice brimmed with excitement.

"I reckon with a little practice you'll be able to shoot twice as good as me, but the first thing you have to learn is how to squeeze the trigger instead of yanking it as if it were a trip rope. That's the reason you missed your shot, Willie, but don't worry, you'll get the next one; it just takes a little practice."

"Where did you get your practice from, Mister Kendell?" Jemima asked.

Her question made him think. Where had he learned to handle a six-shooter and a Winchester? It was not a single event he could put a date on, but an ongoing process, he decided; one which had its start as a boy hunting squirrels with his father in the mountains of Virginia and was continuing even now, in the Arizona deserts . . . hunting men. The layoff in between seemed of little consequence now; his life was flowing again, like a river temporarily stymied by sandbars, and as he looked back over the course of it, the rapids and the still water appeared to blend together in an even flow. It was a valid question, however, and the wide-eyed girl who stared up at him now deserved an answer—though Kendell had no intention of confessing his whole life to this little one.

He looked down at her then gave her a smile. "I suppose I learned to hunt when I was a boy, about Willie's age. Later on when I was not too much older I fought in the war. A war teaches a man more than he'll ever need to know about guns and hunting." It was enough of the truth, without all the embellishments, to satisfy the girl.

"Our pa fought in the war, too," Jemima said. "He used to talk 'bout it sometimes; said he fought with Colonel John Baylor."

"Baylor? Then I reckon your pa and I were on opposite sides of the battlefield."

Jemima shrugged her shoulders. "It don't matter now anyway. That war is long over and Pa said we needed to forget 'bout all our differences and learn to live with one another 'cause we don't need another war to tear our country apart again."

"Sounds like your pa was a wise man, Jemima."

Tears gathered in her bright blue eyes and she nodded her head. "Yes, he was," she said, suddenly burying her face against his side.

"Just cry it out," he told her, putting a hand on her shoulder and knowing exactly how she felt. Willie stood by quietly with the long rifle clutched awkwardly in his arms. When she finished she straightened and wiped her eyes.

"I'm sorry, Mister Kendell," she said in a tiny voice.

"Nothing to be sorry about, Jemima. There's no shame in crying when you're really hurting."

The three continued on and the mood had turned gloomy when suddenly a big jack sprang into the open and shattered their dreary cloud.

Willie struggled with the Henry and Kendell told him to wait for the rabbit to stop and strike a pose. "They always do because their curiosity gets the best of them," Kendell said just as the jack pulled up and sat very still but for its twitching nose sampling the scents on the wind.

"Now remember what I told you; line him up and squeeze the trigger gently and don't even think about anything but keeping him in your sights. The gun will fire when it's ready. Your job is to keep your eye on the target and make sure that the front and rear sights stay lined up properly."

Willie followed instructions well and it seemed an eternity as the trigger crept slowly back. Then the sear released, the hammer struck and the old Henry leaped in the boy's hands.

"I got him! I got him!" Willie cried, running off to claim his trophy. Kendell watched the two children return. Now each carried a rabbit by the ears. Willie marched back with his chest puffed out and for some reason the rifle looked less ungainly hitched under his arm. The boy was a hunter now; he had grown a little that evening, and he knew it.

Glancing at the darkening sky, Kendell said, "Now that we have our meat I'll show you two how to dress it out and cook it over a campfire."

It was well after dark when Kendell peeled off the last shred of meat from the white bones and settled back to enjoy a hot cup of coffee. Even Willie advanced toward the hot black liquid now, and although it was bitter as sin, he drank it down hardily—after all, it was all a part of being grown up; the little boy inside him would have to grow up quickly now that he was on his own.

9

The three women huddled close as the sun went down; an unconscious grouping for comfort, for safety . . . for sympathy. The long, hot day had passed slowly and painfully for them as each in her turn had endured the degrading play of her captor only to be used again by the other. Each, that is, but for Juana, who had become the exclusive property of Jake Sargot—and that proved a worse fate. They had struggled at first, which led to more bruises, but in the end they each succumbed. They gave their bodies, reluctantly, but they did not give their souls and tried not to give the men the pleasures they sought. Who could find pleasure where there was so little life left, and for these three women, little was left to live for but to satisfy a burning hate growing stronger within each of them every minute.

"I will kill that man," Juana whispered and an uncontrollable shudder gripped her slender body. "His great, dirty hands—every time I think of them pawing me I want to die. I hate him!"

Olinda Flores shook her head and her long black hair, knotted and dirty now, whispered softly across her shoulders and over the tattered white muslin blouse which she had pinned back together as best as she could. "They are terrible men, it is true, but we must not hate them. We are God's children; what would the priest think?"

"The priest is dead," Teresa Trezona said bitterly without

looking up. "Who cares what he would think, anyway? These men are not the children of God; they are bastards, fathered by Satan. It is good to hate them; it is God's will that we should hate them—it would have been the Padre's will also."

"Perhaps you are right," Olinda said. "It is much easier to hate them than to love them; they must surely be of Satan." She looked up at Teresa. "I did not know they had killed the priest too," she said in a low voice now edged with a new sorrow.

Teresa nodded her head and lowered it again. "I saw it happen. They killed him in the street, by the church; it was a terrible thing."

"There is no hope for us—only from God."

Teresa's eyes were scornful as they turned sharply upon Olinda. "There will be no help from Him either," she said, looking out across the vast desert (dying slowly with the sun) without really seeing it. "There will be no help for us . . . from anywhere."

"But did not the Indian say . . . ?"

"You live on dreams, Olinda; who in San Pablo could help us? Does your father or brother own a gun? Does Juana's father?" Her laugh was mocking. "If a plow could shoot bullets then maybe my father would rescue us. No, no one will come for us, Olinda." Teresa's eyes turned down to her hands folded upon her lap.

Olinda frowned and looked at Juana. Juana was watching the bearded man and her eyes were not the eyes Olinda ever remembered seeing before. Different now; no longer the warm, mysteriously playful eyes which had turned men to clay—now they were hard and cold and hateful.

She became aware of Olinda's gaze and tipped her head up, whispering, "I will kill that man, and the others. I will kill them all."

"You talk foolishness. How could you hope to do such a thing?" Olinda asked helplessly.

Juana's eyes changed, growing suddenly alive and narrowing as she glanced back at Sargot. Her voice dropped and she leaned close to Olinda, speaking barely above her breath. "He carries a small gun in the top of his boot. I saw it there when he—" She shuddered and her words trailed off as if even mentioning the act he had committed against her was a vile sin. "I saw it," she continued, "and the next time, when he is lying breathless upon the ground"—her mind recoiled at the vision of what she would have to endure—"the next time I will take that gun from his boot and I will kill him with it."

"But then what? Surely you cannot hope to kill all four! They will kill you—"

"I do not care! I do not want to live after this."

"But then they will also kill Teresa and myself. These are violent men—we live only so long as we bring them pleasure." Olinda shook her head. "I do not want to die."

"How could you continue to live with this disgrace?"

"It is not our disgrace, Juana; it is theirs."

Juana did not reply and turned away instead to fix her eyes upon Jake Sargot.

Olinda pondered her words and thought of the man who had ravished her—the skinny one. He had cruel eyes and evil hands and she cringed feeling the pain of them even now as her eyes fell upon his terrible image. He was standing across the sand, leaning against the shady side of a boulder, fondling something in his fingers she could not identify.

Ben Jones looked up, saw the girl watching him and grinned at her. Olinda looked quickly away just as Pedro came up to him glancing at the thing in his hand.

"What you got there?" he asked Jones.

Jones gave him a wide grin and showed him. Pedro's face sagged as he recognized the object and he shook his head. "You're a sick man, Jones," he said, walking away.

Jones laughed. "Hey, they make tobacco pouches and medicine bags out of 'em," he hollered after him. "Ain't that right, Cochise?" he said, shifting his view to the Indian.

Sitting apart from the white men, Cuchillo Rojo chose to ignore him. Jones crossed the sand and stood over him.

"Hey, tell me, Cochise, how do them Indians make these here things into bags? You wait for 'em to dry up first or do you stitch 'em up before they get too hard?"

Cuchillo raised his head slowly to look up into Jones' cold green eyes. The eyes of a snake, he thought, returning his gaze to the large black beetle he had been watching.

"Well?" Jones' voice became impatient.

"Cochise has been dead many years," Cuchillo replied, his head still turned away.

Jones' lips tightened. "Hey, I asked you a question, Indian."

Cuchillo dismissed the beetle, fixing his eyes upon the stiffening slip of skin in Jones' hand. He said, "You are mistaken. The practice was brought to the Indians by the white men—the men who first crossed our land. They were —some were," he corrected himself, "vicious men thinking no more of the Indian than they would a dog—even less.

They first cut up our women, taking the breast for their trinket bags. We learned it from your kind. Later we became very good at it . . . but we do not make medicine bags of them. Medicine bags are sacred. The Apache fight among themselves often, but never have I known of one to do such a thing as you have to one of his own." He looked back at the piece of skin. "You are worse than the Apache which you hate." His words hung in the air a moment, like the stillness before a storm.

Ben Jones' nostrils flared and he reached for Cuchillo, but the Indian was a quick old fox who had known his intentions even before Jones had known them himself. A knife flashed from the top of Cuchillo's moccasin and cold steel pressed suddenly into Jones' throat. He stopped, not daring to move.

"As I have told you"—Cuchillo's words were low and menacing—"Cochise has been dead many years and you are very near to joining him in the world beyond this one."

Ben Jones could only stare up into Cuchillo's coal-black eyes and he was having difficulty breathing against the blade pressing into his throat.

"What the hell is going on here?" Sargot demanded, grabbing Jones by the shoulder and pulling him away from Cuchillo's knife.

"What do we need him with us for anyway, Jake?" Jones snapped back, rubbing at the trickle of blood upon his neck.

Cuchillo returned the knife to his moccasin while Sargot shifted his view from him to Jones, seeing what he was holding. "Put that thing away," he barked, realizing suddenly what had provoked the old Apache. "I don't want to see it again—you savvy, Jones?"

"Why you always sticking up for that redskin?"

"He has ten times the brains you have, that's why."

His green eyes narrowed down to two vicious slits and he reached for the pistol at his side, but something stayed his hand as he noticed for the first time the smile curling Sargot's lips.

"Don't stop now," Sargot chided, "you're just a heartbeat away from making this trip a whole lot easier on me and Pedro."

Sargot's hand lingered by the pistol at his side; Jones was no match for the bearded man and he knew it. He let the challenge drop and stomped away.

Sargot grinned back into Cuchillo's impassive face. "I should have let you finish it. I'll be damned surprised if he makes it to them mountains still breathing."

Cuchillo looked down at the ground, nodding his head. "By morning we will be in the mountains," he replied, once again watching the black beetle's slow progress across the sand. He did not care for Jake Sargot any more than he cared for Jones. Of the three, only Pedro did a fine job of keeping out of his way; Cuchillo appreciated that.

Sargot left him sitting there, rounding up the small group in preparation to push on.

10

The cold moonlight threw a ghostly glow across the desert landscape. Kendell slept at the foot of a boulder, a saddle for a pillow and a blanket to keep him warm. Too many years sleeping under a roof makes it easy for one to forget the habits which had been practiced and drummed into your head. It was easy to settle into a sound sleep when light sleeping was no longer expedient.

The horses coming up made no noise—none that Kendell was aware of, nor was he aware of his own animal pawing nervously, tasting the scents in the air. A dozen years ago Matt Kendell would have been conscious of the Indians when they had stopped atop the dark ridge and he would have welcomed them with a volley of hot lead as they crept into camp. But now, like the two children curled close by, he slept on, blissfully unaware until his blanket was flung off.

Kendell came awake, immediately aware of the situation and reached for the holstered pistol by his head; a leather-covered foot came down upon his wrist. The Indian took the gunbelt, stepping away from him and motioning with the barrel of a percussion rifle for Kendell to stand. He obeyed, regardful of a second Indian who had an arrow fitted to his bow while the third man roused Jemima and Willie, pulling them from their blankets.

No one spoke. The children came awake rubbing their

eyes, looking from the Indians to Kendell. He avoided their gaze. It was his own fault, he told himself. He had known the Indians were somewhere ahead of them and should have guessed all the shooting earlier would have attracted attention—and it didn't take much serious thought, either, to know a fire in the desert can be seen a long way off. Any way he sliced it, it came up weighing heavy on the thoughtless side.

In another moment two figures entered the camp after waiting in the shadows in the event of trouble—how much they had overestimated him, Kendell thought with little humor. One was Indian and pretty much looked like his partners. The old woman, however, stood out like a fifth ace and Jemima's eyes gaped when the old hag came into camp wearing her mother's dress. She made a little sound like a muffled cry and wrapped her arms protectively around Willie, who was standing, wide-eyed also, immediately in front of her.

The Indian passed Kendell's gunbelt to the one with the bow and arrow. The man's eyes gleamed as he drew out the pistol, turning it over in his hand to admire it in the moonlight. The leader rested the ancient rifle in the crook of his arm, took a long moment to consider Kendell and the children, then glanced down at the saddlebags.

"You got whiskey?" His English was broken.

"No," Kendell replied.

The leader made a motion and a brave tore open the saddlebags, spreading their contents upon the ground; taking the jerky, two boxes of 44-40 cartridges and sorting through the rest. He repacked what he wanted, taking the bags, Kendell's Winchester and Willie's Henry rifle back with him to the horses. Kendell watched him impassively.

The Indian with the percussion rifle looked at the two children but spoke to Kendell. "Yours?" he asked.

"No."

He said something in Apache and a brave hauled the two kids off. They put up a struggle but Jemima was too smart a girl to make any serious effort against the Indian. He brought them to where the horses were tied and sat them on the ground.

Then the leader looked back at Kendell, nodding toward the dark rise of the Dragoon Mountains. "Why do you follow the other whites into our mountains?"

Kendell remained silent. The Apache's black eyes searched him closely, but the moonlight was to his back and Kendell couldn't read anything in them through the shadow it cast. One thing he was certain of, though, and that was this Apache didn't have much in the way of patience and what little he did have he was losing quickly.

"Who are they—what do they seek?" he demanded again.

"I don't know what you're talking about," Kendell said.

The rifle butt came around, clipping him solidly on the chin. Kendell levered himself up on one elbow, shaking his head. When he picked himself off the ground, there was fire in his side and he drew his hand away and looked at the blood on his fingers. His chin ached but it was only a secondary annoyance. He straightened painfully to his full height, then the old woman's cackling grated his ears, making his skin crawl.

She nudged the Indian aside and it didn't surprise Kendell that he allowed her to do that; they have a superstition of sorts about her kind. Her eyes bore into his face and her lips screwed up; grotesque lips, sunken in where missing teeth ought to have been to support them.

"My name is Annie," she said, studying him closely, her head tilting like a curious hound. She spread her dress with her fingers and turned a circle to model it for him. "See Annie's new dress?" she continued, spinning like a top as if on display. "You think Annie pretty?"

Kendell glanced at Jemima. The kid was petrified, yet her faithful hand remained latched onto her little brother's arm. Her eyes were lost to the shadows, but he could guess the horrified expression which must be there watching her mother's dress paraded around on this crazy dame's back—well, Annie was sure enough acting crazy that it was what she really was.

Kendell was aware of the grinning Indians around him. She had them convinced she was crazy, and she was doing a fair job at convincing him, too. He had not the slightest notion why she had teamed up with this gang of renegades. Why they put up with having her along was something of a mystery, too. She would, however, prove to be a source of entertainment when their stories got old and the days long and hot and, besides, the Apache harbored some religious notions concerning folks who weren't playing with a full deck. Kendell knew they would not want to take a chance at upsetting any spirits, so they probably let her tag along just because she wanted to. Annie would be a harmless old hag—to them at least.

Now they were enjoying her antics, but they had not let up on their guard, and since they had just acquired three more guns to bolster them, Kendell didn't figure escape was much of a possibility at the moment. The one with his pistol was more interested in his new toy than in Annie; examining it closely and discussing something with a friend who had himself just come into possession of a relatively new '86 Winchester. A third held onto Willie's rifle by the barrel in a nonchalant manner, grasping a long war-lance in his other hand. He and the head honcho with the caplock were watching Kendell, not Annie.

She stopped her twirling and leaned close to him. "Annie will dance for you if you give her gold."

"I don't have any gold," Kendell said.

Something changed in her eyes, sharpening up a bit and peering closely at him. They suddenly seemed to burn as they studied him intently and then she turned away, moving back by the horses. In another moment Annie spun back around, cackling like a sorceress about to cast a spell, and then the show was over and the Indians came back at him.

The boss man stalked around Kendell, pushed him up against the rock and said, "You will tell me about the white men ahead."

"I don't think so," Kendell said. The rifle started up again and then stopped. The grin on the Indian's face made Kendell grow cold. He spoke in Apache to the one holding the war-lance and Willie's rifle. The man leaned his weapons against a boulder, knelt by the smoldering remains of the campfire and fed twigs into it, blowing on the coals until a flame leaped to life. Kendell glanced back at the head honcho, not liking the look of the smile that twisted his lips. He wasn't sure what these *renegados* had in mind for him, but whatever it was, he was certain it wasn't the fixings of a pleasant evening.

Annie stood close to the children and Kendell wondered what thoughts might be racing through Jemima's brain. Her eyes held the old woman in a frozen stare and if a little child was capable of knowing real hate, Jemima was feeling it now. But Kendell didn't think so. Hate just wasn't in the natural makeup of children. It was one of those finer qualities of the human animal which had to be learned—well, school was in session and Jemima was learning a lesson which would shape the rest of her life. He found that notion slightly disconcerting, but salved his concerned conscious by reminding himself that the rest of her life wasn't likely to amount to much more than a few hours.

It was almost dark when Jake Sargot swung up onto his horse and started the little group moving toward the black peaks rising ahead in a long, ragged wall. He turned in the saddle to study Cuchillo, who was still down below gazing off into the distance.

"What's that fool Indian up to now?" Ben Jones grumbled.

Sargot frowned and rode down to the Apache.

"What is it?"

Cuchillo read the concern in Sargot's eyes. "Can you not hear it?" he asked.

"Hear what?" Sargot's voice was skeptical as he looked into the old Indian's lined face. He turned his eyes in the direction Cuchillo had been looking.

In a moment Cuchillo said, "There . . . rifle shots. Many miles away."

"I don't hear nothing."

It was true. Cuchillo smiled inwardly at this thought; the

white man has ears yet he does not hear, he has eyes and he does not see.

"Are you sure?"

Cuchillo nodded his head. "They are gunshots."

Sargot regarded him with suspicion. "Well, if you're right we need to be making tracks."

Cuchillo turned his horse and followed Sargot back to the waiting riders. The women were there, hands again tied to the saddles and looking more tired than he remembered seeing them. They had been given no time to rest and Cuchillo regretted their ordeal but it was the affair of the white men and he was only along to guide them to a place of safety—and when they reached it, what then? Perhaps he would leave at that time. He did not think Sargot would permit that, nor did he think remaining among these men would be wise, for they would not want to let anyone live who could point an accusing finger at them for their evil deeds. Cuchillo was mildly amused at the thought that they would try and stop him from leaving as if they might be able to stop a spirit from melting into the dark. This was his land; his home. At any time he could be gone. It was no task at all to slip away from these men who knew not the desert, and now he gave the idea some consideration.

He thought of the rider coming up behind them. Cuchillo wasn't certain, of course, but he had an idea as to who it might be. Perhaps he would just slip quietly away and watch the outcome from afar—or perhaps he'd circle back and lend the devil a hand, although Cuchillo was certain his help would be unneeded, and most likely unwanted, when the time came for evening up old scores.

11

The more Matt Kendell pondered on it, the more he was convinced there was really no good reason why he should not tell these renegades all about the men he was trailing, and what they had done in San Pablo—no good reason except his own stubbornness and a deep-felt personal need to keep the hate he knew toward them bottled up and safe inside him. Not that he felt his story would somehow turn the hearts of these men, sending them charging off to right the wrong that had been committed on San Pablo. The plain truth of it was that it wouldn't change their plans one bit, so why give them the satisfaction of hearing it from his lips.

Well, that was his line of thinking at first, and it had been a firm line as they had turned their attention from him to building up the fire. He couldn't follow their conversation and he didn't figure that was really important anyway. What was important was the fact he was well guarded and he couldn't have gotten anywhere very fast on foot even if he did get away. Besides, if he did he'd have to leave Jemima and Willie behind, and for some reason that notion now put a hobble on any plan he might come up with. He tried to tell himself they were just excess baggage, just two millstones that prevented him from accomplishing what needed doing—well, he tried, despite the fact that it had suddenly become outdated information. It was unfortunate, but somewhere along the line he had developed a genuine interest in the welfare of these two homeless waifs.

He watched the fire grow crackling hot, and it wasn't much time after that that he gathered a fair notion as to what was brewing in their twisted brains. About the time they buried the long, iron point of the war-lance in the bed of coals Kendell began having second thoughts as to how sacred the information he was carrying really was.

Minutes passed and Kendell found it difficult to pull his eyes from that glowing spear point, but he managed a glance at the two children huddled together by the horses. They were no threat to the Indians and they were treated as such. Sitting there with that Indian standing over them, Jemima and Willie did not appear as if they were planning to go anywhere, and if they did figure a way to sneak off, it would be no real problem to find them again.

Annie came near and peered down at Kendell. This time her eyes were clear and precise as they flashed over him. Then she knelt down beside him and said in a low voice, "I can get you out of this pot of stew, you know." Her eyes narrowed and she glanced over her shoulder. "They listen to me; they think I'm crazy."

"That seems to be the general opinion and I don't see you doing much to change it."

She laughed, and it wasn't the high cackling laugh either, but low and guarded. "Why do you think I'm talking to you now? You already think I'm crazy. Now I'm here to tell you I ain't. Besides, what do you think my life would be worth if I let them savages think otherwise?"

Kendell shrugged his shoulders. "It doesn't appear they're keeping you by force."

"Keeping me?" Annie said with a note of humor revealing itself in her voice. She dragged a hand across her nose, sniffing. "It's more like the other way around, mister."

"I had it figured you were with them by choice, only it was just too incredible a notion to believe."

"Well, believe it, mister. I'm here because right now this is where I want to be."

"For what good reason?"

"Like I said, I can get you out of this bad luck you've seemed to come upon—you and those kids," and she grinned at Kendell, rubbing her thumb and forefinger together in a gesture understood in most languages.

"You're here for money?"

"Of course I am, what other reason could there be? You don't think I like being the butt of their jokes, do you? I know what them damned savages think of me. Hell, let them think what they please so long as there's a profit in it for me. Look at me, mister, what do you see? A old lady what ain't got no chance at getting the finer things life has to offer; the things it takes money to buy. I want them things. Listen, you know right now there's a fellow in Europe somewheres who's building a thing the papers are calling a 'horseless carriage.' His name is Benz and he calls his horseless carriage a 'Victoria.' I seen a picture of it in a Denver newspaper a few years back and decided right then and there I was going to have me a Victoria!"

Annie's eyes twinkled with a sudden excitement and she stretched out her arms holding pretend reins. "Can you imagine old Annie riding about in one of them Victorias without no horses up front loud-bucking in her face or droppin' smelly road apples as she rides along on her way? Yep, that would make me one fancy lady, it would."

Annie's arms fell back to her sides and her eyes grew indistinct. "And there are other things, too. Pretty clothes, fancy houses back east where you don't have to tote the water or have a privy out back. It's all inside now—they've got them things now, you know?" Her voice trailed off and she looked back at Kendell.

"Where's the profit now?" he said, looking at her from under his brows.

A scowl clouded her eyes. "Don't appear to be any—leastways none for old Crazy Annie. Not unless you got some gold coins hidden on you somewheres and are willing to part with them to save your hide—and theirs, heh?"

"I said I don't have any money, Annie, and that's the truth."

She shrugged her shoulders and made an effort to stand, saying, "No profit for Annie tonight."

"Where was the profit in that sodbuster's homestead you burned out yesterday?"

Annie stopped and squatted back down. "How do you know about that?" she inquired, studying Kendell closely.

"I was there."

"No you weren't. There was no one else around, we checked. You can't know who did it."

"You aren't denying it."

"No, of course I ain't . . . only, how do you know?"

Kendell nodded at the two kids. "It was their home, their mother and father you murdered. That dress you're wearing belonged to her mother; she's wearing the mate to it."

Annie squinted at Jemima and looked back at Kendell, grinning. "So it is. Don't know how we missed them two."

"Their mother put them in hiding before you and your friends swooped down on them."

"Well, it ain't important."

"It is to them. They lost their parents and their home. Did you make much of a profit on that raid?"

"I got me a new dress, didn't I? Also got a pouch of gold from the top bureau drawer." She made a toothless grin. "Yeah, I'd say I made out all right."

"And they paid the price."

"No one ever said life was all hog fat. If it weren't so hard, don't you think I'd find a different way to scratch out a livin' from it?"

"No," Kendell said dryly after a brief moment of consideration.

Annie pushed the scowl from her face and cackled again. It was a good touch; the Indians were becoming curious about their conversation. She started to rise again and Kendell stopped her with a question.

"I'm curious about one thing, Annie."

"Heh—?"

"How can you come up with any profit running with a gang of thieves like them? It seems to me you'd be fighting tooth and nail just to keep a share of the take."

Annie shook her head. "You don't know Injuns, mister." She paused looking at him. "Say, what is your name, anyway, mister?"

"Kendell, Matt Kendell."

"Kendell . . . ? Seems to me I heard of a Kendell once

afore." She studied him, then said, "Naw, couldn't be you, though."

"You were about to teach me something which I didn't know about Indians," Kendell prompted.

Annie shook a puzzled look from her face and said, "Like I was tellin' you, Kendell, you don't know them Injuns. They ain't got no sense of priorities; their values are all siderailed onto a spur what don't go nowhere but to a bottle. Like that squatter's place we hit yesterday. Hell, the first thing they looked for was a bottle of whiskey, and when they didn't find any they got all upset and commenced to breaking things. Next they looked for guns—well, 'fraid they came up empty-handed on both accounts yesterday. But not old Crazy Annie. Why, the first place I hit is the drawers and cabinets 'cause I know that's where most folks keep their pouches. Hell, Kendell, them red bastards don't give two hoots 'bout gold—or nothin' what's important to a white man."

A smile twisted her ugly lips and her laugh was only a notch shy of the cackle she did so well. "Know what really tickles them Injuns, heh? Know what them boys will trade whiskey and guns for? And a mountain of gold if'n they had any to trade?" Her eyebrows hitched up expectantly.

"Why don't you tell me, Annie?" Kendell said when her pause dragged out.

"Parrot feathers! Yeah, that's what I said, parrot feathers, or eagle feathers; it don't make much difference to them. Feathers are religious, or something, and they'd swap you a whole pouch full of gold for a few lousy feathers!" She laughed again. "And they think old Annie is crazy."

Annie stood and moved away from him, pausing briefly

between the savages and the children to throw a glance at Jemima and Willie, breaking out suddenly with one of her cackles.

A cold-hearted bitch, and Kendell wasn't so certain she wasn't crazy after all. She stood hunched over, filling out the blue gingham dress like a badly molded lump of clay, and her appearance was even more repulsive than when she was near. He had a notion Annie would be right at home on a dark October night—just give the little lady a broomstick, he mused, trying not to think of the glowing spear point waiting in the coals. That was something else . . .

It wasn't a particularly warm night, in fact it was downright cool, as nights in the desert under clear skies often are. Despite that, Kendell was aware of the sweat beading up on his forehead. The children had not stirred and Annie had finally sat herself down by the fire. One of the Indians, the one who was now the proud owner of an '86 Winchester, rose to his feet and returned to his post by the children. He just stood over them, watching, and Kendell figured that whatever they were planning was about to soon begin and they didn't want any interference from a couple of clawing, biting, kicking kids.

The ringleader returned, standing over him and grinning. One front tooth was missing and the other badly chipped. Out of the corner of his eye Kendell watched Jemima squirming where she was sitting and then lean over to whisper something in Willie's ear. The little boy's head jerked up and his eyes fixed on Annie. The man standing behind them, cradling the Winchester in his arm, wasn't paying the kids any attention; his attention was directed at what was about to occur in the center ring.

Kendell looked up at the Indian hovering over him. "The answer is still the same," he told him.

Now the Indian smiled broadly. "But I have not asked a question," he said, motioning for another sitting by the fire to come. The Indians had changed rules in midgame and Kendell didn't think that was quite fair. It was an easy thing to start off brave, if for no other reason than to retain a semblance of pride, and then back down later, telling them all they wanted to know and allowing them the feeling of victory when the going got really rough. But now when they didn't give him any place to back down to—well, he didn't figure he liked these new rules very much.

The second Indian grabbed Kendell's arms and pressed a knee into his back.

Kendell put muscle into it but the one who held him had him locked down real good; he figured a rope could not have done a better job of it and this way they had more control over him; able to move him into any position that would suit their needs.

"After we are finished here we will go see for ourselves what the other white men want in our mountains."

"Your mountains?"

But the Indian wasn't buying any of Kendell's attempts to postpone the inevitable with talk. "They have always been our mountains," he replied turning away.

Kendell put more muscle into it but the man behind him just clamped down tighter. Kendell let up, conserving what strength he had.

Annie was watching him with a sparkle in her eye and a toothless smile on her lips. It didn't take a whole lot to amuse some folks, he thought, looking briefly at the children. Jemima's eyes were wide with fear—or maybe it was horror, and Kendell regretted the kids having to witness what was about to happen.

Then the Indian returned, carrying the war-lance, and in the darkness the glowing blade came alive. He stood over him with it while the man behind him buried his knee deeper into his back, pulling harder on his arms until Kendell's elbows came together.

Suddenly all Matt Kendell could see was that red-hot iron dancing in front of his face, and the ache which up to now had filled his heart, for the moment did not seem quite as intolerable as he had once imagined it to be.

"You are bleeding," the Indian observed, seeing the blood on Kendell's shirt. "I can stop it," and he put the tip of the spear to the open wound. The woolen shirt smoked and skin and blood hissed as the iron pressed down. Kendell threw back his head, grinding his teeth, and the stench of burning flesh filled the air.

Annie was doing a little jig out on the sand and clapping her hands as she danced. Kendell saw her only vaguely through eyes already clouding from the pain. When the burning point was pulled away, he collapsed, breathing heavily, his eyes further blurred by the sweat streaming off his brow.

"The bleeding is stopped, see," the Indian said, quite unabashedly pleased with himself, and the glowing iron moved toward another patch of skin.

12

Sargot threw up his arm and in the paling moonlight the party came to a halt. The air was cool now and easy traveling for the horses; they shifted beneath their burdens, anxious to continue on. He turned in his saddle to survey the group and the long trail behind them melting into the shadows of the desert night. The three women nodded in their saddles, half asleep, half awake while Ben Jones and Pedro waited a few paces behind them with the mule in tow.

Sargot's eyes lingered a moment on that mule and the pack it was carrying. It did his heart good to see the bulging tarp tied across those packs; the church had been rich with gold—gold chalices, gold plates, even the bells upon the altar had been gold. And the priest's vestments had been painstakingly embroidered with gold thread. Sargot had taken those too. He had taken everything that had gleamed yellow and had caught his eye, and now the church's gold was his gold. Once in Mexico it would buy him all the power and men he would need to come back across the border and do it all over again. There were hundreds of little villages like San Pablo with hundreds of little churches. Perhaps none as rich—but there was riches in volume.

The sight and the thought pleased him. Glancing along their trail, all appeared to be in order—at least as far as he could discern. The Apache's warning had troubled him at first, but so far the only evidence of approaching danger had been the Indian's word—and some damned feeling the old man had in his bones. He scoffed at that idea now. He had been running scared because of some old man's arthritis—Indian superstition crap, he thought, looking across at Cuchillo.

"Well," he said, "which way from here?"

For the last hour the ground had changed, growing steeper and more rocky, with the sand of the Sonoran Desert thinning out, exposing bedrock, becoming patchy in places and in spots disappearing altogether.

Cuchillo lifted his eyes to the dark rise of land ahead. The trail was steep and the mountain loomed in the blackness beyond. It looked to be less of a mountain than it had appeared ten miles back, but that was because they were already upon its back, viewing only the steep rise of land in the moonlight and not the peaks beyond. The size of the Dragoons was deceitful, as the size of any mountain range is once you have left the flatland and foothills behind and actually pushed a trail up into them.

This place was familiar. Being here again, back in the land of his youth and his beloved leader, Cochise, Cuchillo felt a sudden surge of excitement; a feeling he kept hidden. The trail was old and seldom used anymore, but even in the darkness Cuchillo's eyes read it like a well-worn thoroughfare. It was the same trail he and his young bride, Sun Rising, had followed the first time they came to the stronghold. That had been many, many years ago, yet the vision of her strong, angular face remained as clear in his memory as if it had been that morning.

They were still many miles from the place where a hidden

trail branched off, disappearing into a jumble of rocks—a place where the most experienced trackers could spend days riding in circles. But now Cuchillo would have no difficulty finding it, even if there had been no moonlight at all to show the way.

He allowed his dark eyes to scan the landscape. He felt twenty years younger. Jake Sargot grew impatient beside him.

"Well? You can still find it, can't you?"

Cuchillo smiled at him and spoke no words, for the smile said it all.

Sargot took a drink from the canteen. "How long?"

"Two . . . maybe three hours."

Pedro and Jones rode up to them and Jones said, "Hey, how much longer we got to stay in these saddles?"

"Your butt getting sore?"

"Yeah, Jake, ain't yours?"

"Hell no; I'm a hardass!"

Pedro moved between the two of them and said, "Why don't we take a few minutes and stretch our legs, heh?"

Cuchillo agreed. "We have time; I do not think he can follow us once we are into Cochise's stronghold." He was suddenly in no hurry to bring these men into the sacred place—well, it was not really a sacred place to the Indians, not like the hidden burial grounds which were near the stronghold, but Cuchillo was now considering that the stronghold should be reserved for the Indians only, and that being so, it suddenly became sacred. Yet he had promised he would lead these men to the stronghold, to the safety it offered, and he would keep his word . . . but that was all. Honesty was not a trait these men possessed, and although it was an important characteristic to Cuchillo, he did not think he had to deal honestly with them now.

"All right," Sargot said, "we'll take a break," and he swung off his saddle.

Olinda Flores came awake, lifting her chin from her chest and looking around. "Why have we stopped?" she asked softly.

Juana looked at her. "I think we are resting here for a little while."

Teresa nudged her horse closer to the two girls. "I am so thirsty. Why do they not give us some water?"

Juana turned a hateful eye to the men, allowing it to burn upon Sargot. Bitterness choked her words. "They only water the horses twice a day; are we any more important to them than their animals?"

"Juana," Olinda said gently, "it will all work out in God's own way. We must bear this cross—"

"You are too trusting—too timid; you are a fool! It will only work according to *their* will . . . or ours, whichever is strongest," and her words seemed to swallow themselves.

"Ours?" Teresa derided. "I wonder who really is the fool, Juana. We can do nothing to change our plight. We have no will here, no weapons with which to fight these men!"

Now Juana's eyes changed; the vehement hate left with a flash of her dark lashes and they became cold and cunning —the same eyes Olinda remembered seeing earlier that evening. "But I have a plan," she whispered.

Teresa laughed. "Yes, you have a plan. Olinda has told me of your plan, and of the little gun. It is a plan to get us all killed!"

"You find that terrible?"

Teresa remained sullen.

"I for one do not care to die," Olinda reminded Juana.

"I welcome death," Juana said, distracted, and then she added with sudden zeal, "but my plan does not require our deaths—only the death of those pigs!"

"Olinda told me of the little gun in Sargot's boot and how you intend to get it from him. Even if you did succeed, even if you did somehow get your hands on it and killed him, you could not kill the other three. If only one remains alive he will kill us all!"

"You are mistaken, Teresa," Juana said. "There will not be three, but only two. You've seen how the Indian acts; he cares nothing for them as he cares nothing for us. He will not revenge their deaths upon us."

Teresa laughed sarcastically. "So, we have only two to worry over. They might as well be two hundred! They have guns and knives, and all you will have when you are finished with Sargot is one empty gun. Your plan is a leaking sieve, Juana, and it *will* get us killed."

Juana shook her head. "Listen to me, there are three of them and three of us. We can do it but you two must help me."

"Help?" Olinda said.

"Yes."

"But how can we?"

"By using yourselves to distract them. Olinda, the skinny one with the foul breath and that ugly knife, he favors you. And Teresa, you must make Pedro want you too. I . . . I will make Sargot spend much time with me . . ." She cringed to think of how she would have to act—to perform for that beast to keep his attention, but she would do it. The hate she felt would make the unbearable bearable.

Olinda shook her head convulsively. "No, you can't mean that we are to invite them to . . ." She could not finish the sentence.

"That is exactly what I mean, and you must be within reach of their weapons and you must kill them—you must! It is the only way we can free ourselves!"

Teresa thought this over a moment while watching Juana's face in the thin, cold moonlight, then very slowly she nodded her head. "Yes . . . I think it might work, but it is very daring."

"Daring and cunning are the only weapons we have."

Olinda was still shaking her head. "I will not—can not offer myself to that man!"

Teresa wished she could reach out a hand and console her, but the ropes that secured them prevented that. Instead she tried to reach out with words. "Olinda, I know it is a terrible thing to contemplate, but we will have to do it if we want to ever leave alive—you keep saying you don't want to die."

"I just don't think I will be able."

"Listen, we must strike out and strike hard. Besides, Olinda, what more can you lose than they have already taken from you? They have taken your pride and your virginity; do not sacrifice your life to them as well."

Olinda looked helplessly at her. "But what will God think of such a deed—killing is wrong!"

"When a dog becomes mad it must be destroyed. These men are worse than mad dogs for they are fully aware of what they do. Olinda, it is not wrong to kill when it is to preserve your life, or another's."

"If only I could speak with the priest. He always had the right advice . . ."

"The Padre is dead. I have told you this already—forget him," Teresa admonished.

"The Padre would have blessed us in this, Olinda," Juana added gently.

"Do you really think so?"

"Yes, I do."

Olinda drew a deep breath and allowed it to escape slowly, nodding her head. "I will do it then," and when she looked back at Juana, Juana was looking past her in a stare wide as death. Olinda turned around and a gasp caught in her throat. Cuchillo was there astride his horse. She looked quickly back to Juana with fear torturing her fine young face.

Did he hear? The question screamed in Juana's brain.

The girls became silent and a feeling of doom settled about them. Cuchillo urged his horse nearer with an expressionless face and black eyes that pierced to their hearts. "I have brought you water," he said to them.

Juana watched him closely as he gave each of them a drink. *Did he hear? He must have heard their plans, but why doesn't he say something . . . perhaps he did not hear?* The uncertainty tortured her.

Cuchillo capped the canteen and rejoined the white men. They saddled up and the group continued along the trail only Cuchillo could follow. As they neared Cochise's stronghold, Cuchillo was aware of that feeling again. He was twenty years younger and twenty years stronger; he could hear the mountains whispering a heartfelt and long-overdue welcome home to him. Outside, he remained impassive. Inside, his heart rejoiced. Then he knew the reason he had agreed to lead these men here. It had been obscured at first, clouded by other feelings and other needs, but now it was clear as a mountain lake. He agreed to lead them into the Dragoons so that he too could once again climb the mountain of his fathers; he was an old man and he was coming home.

He rode on and a faint smile touched his lips and then died. Now something else was in the air and he became rigid in the saddle. It was the Devil's Wind, and as the mountains had done earlier, it too was whispering to him.

The whisper was a mere feeling in his bones, but it spoke to him in words, words which rang throughout his being: *I am coming,* it said to him, and Cuchillo knew a time of reckoning was soon to be at hand.

13

Kendell seemed to recall reading somewhere that supposedly your whole life flashes before your eyes when you finally stare death in the face and take that last fatal step toward eternity. Well, he figured he was staring at death now—death in the form of a glowing, iron-tipped Apache war-lance, but the events of his life, so far, had remained buried in the past and all he was really aware of was the searing pain in his side and the fire of hate consuming him like the Devil's own hell. The war-lance danced near and struck out with the sting of a rattlesnake.

Kendell recoiled, squirming under the lance's own peculiar variety of venom, and flinched when the Indian pulled it away. He was only vaguely aware of the smoldering patch of wool at his shoulder.

In a distracted, disassociated sort of way, Kendell found himself able to step back and view the scene as if he were completely detached. In his mind he walked out among the Indians, studying each carefully, as if browsing casually along the corridors of a wax museum. Between the burning strikes, time seemed to stand still, and the idea that he had already been driven crazy with the pain amused him—crazy, just like old Annie. But what concerned him most was not going mad, nor was it the torture of the hot iron, but rather the notion that now he would never complete his mission. His brain brought San Pablo back and that was good; the hate sustained him.

Another strike brought him back to the reality of pain and the grinning faces around him. He tried again to twist free and collapsed, breathing heavily. By the fire, Annie was hopping up and down clapping her hands in glee.

"Kill him . . . kill him," she was singing, twirling in a frantic frenzy. *The hell she wasn't crazy!* Then a movement at the corner of his eye drew his attention.

Willie was standing slowly and peering down at Jemima with a confused, almost helpless look upon his face. She was urging him on to do something and he wasn't quite certain he liked whatever it was. The Indian guarding them was fully enjoying Kendell's distress, and for the present had dismissed the kids from mind.

"Kill him . . . stick it in him!" Annie cackled. Kendell's torturer scowled at the old crow; he wasn't ready for the fun to end . . . not just yet . . . there was still a lot of skin left to burn and the night was far from over.

The point moved again; the bright orange glow had disappeared from it but there was still enough heat left to cause pain.

But before it could strike again the Indian turned away. At the sound which had distracted the Indian, Kendell's eyes went back to Willie. The boy was headlong into a charge, his arms waving in the air, heading straight for Annie.

He threw himself into the old lady. "You killed my mommy!" he cried over and over again, while his arms swung like pistons and his feet like battering rams. Annie hobbled backward rubbing her shin and cursing—but the lad was no match for an adult, even a very old female adult.

Annie picked him up, tossing him aside. "You get away from me!" she screeched, turning to confront the boy. "Get away from me or I'll kill you, too!"

Willie was up like a caged polecat beating at the old woman. Her backhand sent him sprawling.

For the moment their attention turned away from Kendell for the more interesting display taking place by the fire, but Matt Kendell knew the real drama was being acted out a dozen paces away. Willie was only a little tyke, but he was acting out his part like a seasoned thespian; meanwhile, the director of the play was standing offstage about to make her entrance. Kendell shifted his view to Jemima and prepared himself to move quickly when the opening came.

Jemima inched quietly away from the Indian guarding her. He had other things to occupy his attention now. The Henry rifle leaned against the rock where it had been left. She made her way slowly while Willie sidestepped and dodged around the old lady's lunges. Then Jemima was there and grabbing up the rifle levering in a shell like a pro.

"Willie!" she shouted and the boy fell to the ground as if he had rehearsed the part a dozen times. Annie turned with a bewildered look upon her face, saw Jemima put the rifle to her shoulder and swing the barrel her way. The rifle barked, leaping up and Annie flinched at the sound of the bullet whistling past her ear. Jemima cranked down the lever and yanked it up again.

The shot had turned all their heads and in the sudden confusion the Indian behind him let up slightly. Kendell was ready for it. Perhaps the Indian had thought he was too weak to make a break, or perhaps he had just been taken by surprise like the rest of them and wanted to make sure he could hit the sand if Jemima decided to swing the rifle in his direction. In either case, it was enough of a break for Kendell—more than he had hoped for. A sharp, sudden twist broke the Indian's grip and the next instant he had his hand on his revolver, which the Indian was wearing, pulling it from the holster.

The one with the war-lance spun around thrusting the weapon, burying the point of it in the sand as Kendell rolled out from under it, firing. The Apache lurched backward, landing on the ground while his partner turned and skedaddled with the empty holster flapping at his side.

Another shot rang out—a rifle shot and it wasn't the voice of the Henry. The bullet screamed with a high-pitched wavering sound as it ricocheted off the boulder behind him. Kendell turned to see the Indian with his '86 frantically working at the lever. But lever guns were something of a novelty to the man and he didn't quite have the technique down yet. He struggled with the piece an instant longer than fate would allow. Kendell drew a bead and fired. The slug met its mark.

Annie was screeching, running like an old hen across the sand; Kendell let her go as his eyes made a sweep of the camp. The Henry went off again, a more subdued report than his Winchester had made, but he couldn't take the time to see what the result was as a movement in the shadows outside of camp, beyond the reach of firelight, riveted his attention. He swung toward it and his pistol barked; a foot of flame leaped from the muzzle into the darkness and a cry reached his ear. A figure dropped. A poorly released arrow went whizzing overhead.

In his mind he ticked them off—three down, one to go—the one who had hightailed it away as the shooting began. Now he listened as he hunkered up against the rocks. The night grew quiet except for the sounds of a skirmish to his left. Annie and Jemima were going at it now. Kendell tried to rise to his feet but the pain of burned and stretching skin forced him to sit back down.

Suddenly Jemima let out with a terrifying scream. Annie had the girl's arms pinned under her old, bony knees and was lifting a melon-size boulder above her head with both hands. "I'll finish you off now, you little fool!" she hissed, targeting the rock at Jemima's head.

Willie was hopping around not knowing which way to turn and Kendell knew how it was going to end. He struggled to get up but it was taking just too damned long and in another second Jemima would have the life crushed out of her.

"Annie!" Kendell shouted but the old woman ignored him. He turned his pistol on her and fired. The slug hit her with a dull thud and Annie let out a cry, falling off the girl; the rock hit the ground beside Jemima's head. Jemima crawled out from beneath the old woman's body, shrinking away from it, standing and shaking uncontrollably while her eyes remained huge and fixed.

Kendell pulled himself painfully to his feet. One of the Apaches was still alive and lurking somewhere in the shadows, out there just waiting. He made a careful survey of the camp, marking the positions of the bodies. The horses were sidestepping nervously, tugging at their halter ropes; two of them had broken away.

He checked the bodies. The one outside the camp still clutched a bow in his lifeless hand—in death the eyes stared up at the cold, cloudless sky beneath the desert stars. He left him and retrieved his rifle from the other Indian who had been standing guard over the children—he was gratifyingly dead also. Kendell went back to the fellow who had made him squirm under the war-lance, turned him over with the toe of his boot and noted that his bullet had neatly put out the Apache's left eye, exiting through the rear of the skull, leaving a large, ragged hole. He looked at the body and despite what the Indian had done to him, he was surprised he did not take any pleasure in seeing him dead.

Jemima came to him and Kendell turned the child away. "It's best you don't look on this, Jemima," he said to her.

"Are you all right?"

"I have felt better," he said, forcing a smile to his lips.

"You're looking ill, Mister Kendell."

He looked at the bodies strewn around. "It has been a bad evening, Jemima."

"We need to tend to them burns."

"Unless you can find some lard, or know a trick or two I don't, there isn't much we can do for them here and now."

"We have some water to wash them off with."

"No, we'll need to conserve what water we have, and besides, that hot blade most likely killed anything that would infect it."

Jemima frowned and Kendell put a hand on the girl's shoulder. "Thanks, but the best we can do is leave them alone." She was hell-bent on seeing he was taken care of and he felt a little guilty refusing her help; however, at the moment he had more pressing things on his mind—in particular, one Chiricahua Apache who had managed to slip through his fingers. He scanned the black landscape but the Apache would keep out of sight until he was ready to make his strike.

"Jemima!" Willie called out.

They turned and Willie was kneeling beside Annie. "She is still alive," he said, standing.

Kendell knelt down and turned the old lady over. Her head rolled back and her eyelids fluttered open. She looked up at Kendell and a smile came briefly to her lips.

"You're a lucky one," she spoke softly. Kendell let her talk. "I didn't figure you'd be seeing the sun of another day."

"I hadn't counted on it either."

"Don't reckon I'll ever be getting that Victoria now."

Jemima gave Kendell a puzzled look.

"I reckon not, Annie."

She laughed. "Maybe the Devil will have one I can ride—I was sure looking forward to a carriage what ain't had no dirty horses to foul it up." She coughed. "What do you suppose hell will be like?"

Kendell didn't answer her. He had a pretty good idea but didn't figure she needed to be troubled with it now.

"Are they all dead?" she asked him.

"All but one. He got away."

She smiled again. "Well, then maybe you ain't so lucky after all." A spasm of coughing brought up blood. She raised a hand to wipe her lips but had not the strength. "You'll all wind up dead by morning, anyway," she continued fighting for breath. "You see, they got this notion 'bout crazy folks. It's bad medicine to go and kill a fool like me—that's why I made 'em believe I was crazy—I'm not, you know, not really," and her eyes grew intense.

"I know, Annie," Kendell said, and it seemed to satisfy her.

She grinned at him. "I was as safe as a bird in a nest with a flock of momma birds to watch over me. Now that you went and killed me that one left alive will have to avenge my death or face the anger of his gods." She wheezed, gasping for air.

In a moment she went on, saying, "Them Injun boys had a lot of crazy superstitions like that. Never did understand their ways, but one thing I know, as long as that one is alive, he'll have but one thing in his head and that will be to kill you." Those words brought a smile to her lips as if she somehow found comfort in them.

Kendell let her down slowly and the smile remained frozen in death.

"Is she speaking the truth?" Jemima asked.

"I don't know."

Kendell looked down at the old woman for a moment and then stood up, aware of an old feeling he had not known for many years. He stared at the pistol in his hand and thrust it into his belt, glancing at the bodies which lay twisted in death. It was one of the reasons he had given up the gun in the first place, why he had tried to change his life—well, it hadn't taken he reminded himself, so he just better damned well get used to the feeling of disgust that went along with killing—he had a lot more of it to do.

"Let's round up the horses. You and Willie stay near to me; I don't want either of you getting jumped."

"Then you do believe her."

Kendell drew a long breath and let it out slowly. "Yeah, I guess I do."

Jemima called Willie and put an arm around the boy's shoulders when he came near. "You stay close to me—hear?"

"Yeah, sis," he replied, more confused than frightened.

The horses which had broken free and scattered had not gone very far and in a short time Kendell retrieved them, singling out Annie's horse. It carried a tote sack tied behind the cantle. He removed it, dumped the contents on the ground and dug out two pokes of gold coins.

He handed them to Jemima. "Here, these are yours. At least one of them came from your folks but take them both, you'll need them; I'm afraid it's all your Ma and Pa can leave you now."

She took the money, struggling a moment with a tear, but winning the battle and pulling herself up straight and proud. "Thank you," she said.

Kendell gathered up his belongings that the Indians had strewn about the ground and wished he had a holster for his gun, but that had fled along with the Indian who had been wearing it. He saddled up their horses.

"Shouldn't we bury them or something, Mister Kendell?" Jemima said.

"Just let them be."

"But we can't just let the animals get at them."

"That's what the animals are here for, and these four won't care anyway."

"That ain't Christian."

"I haven't got a shovel and I'm in no mood to scratch out graves with my fingers, not now—not with a mad Apache out there somewhere just waiting for a chance to lift my scalp. Now climb up in that saddle and I don't want to hear any more about it. At least you two will have your own horses to ride from here on."

Jemima looked down at the bodies still lying where they had fallen. "But—" she started.

"But nothing!" Kendell barked, suddenly angry. It was an anger which surprised him as much as it startled Jemima. "Climb up on that damned animal or I'll leave you here." His body ached all over, it was true, and he was tired, but that was no reason to fly off the handle at her. He could not explain his reaction, but deep inside he suspected it had something to do with all the killing of the last few days. He had had a bellyful of death and it didn't seem to be getting any easier to swallow.

Jemima's eyes grew hard, narrowing, and she turned around and marched to her horse, stretching her leg up to the tall stirrup to climb awkwardly into the saddle.

Kendell lifted Willie onto another horse, then, looking at Jemima, said, "Hey, I reckon I haven't told you thanks for what you and Willie did this evening. It was mighty bold of you two."

Jemima looked down at him from the saddle and remained silent.

"Well, I reckon I owe you one."

She looked away. "You don't owe us nothing, Mister Kendell, let's just call it even now," and she nudged her horse away from him, pulling up alongside her brother.

Kendell wanted to frown and grin at the same time. Jemima wasn't the same little girl he had picked up the day before. She and Willie had done some mighty fast growing up these last twenty-four hours and he figured by the time their journey was over—if she lived that long—young Jemima Butler would be a force to reckon with in her own right.

He reloaded his six-shooter and wedged it back under his belt, pumped as many .44-40s into his Winchester as the weapon would eat and finally climbed cautiously onto his horse, trying not to injure anything that was already hurting, which amounted to practically everything. Once up in the saddle, he straightened up and readjusted the pistol in his belt. It was an uncomfortable manner in which to carry the piece, but for the moment he didn't have many options. He preferred to carry the Winchester now. Annie's dire warning weighed heavy with him and he wanted the weapon out and ready where he could use it in an instant's warning.

Jemima avoided his eyes when he looked back at her. Well, she'd get over it, she'd have to if she ever wanted to get out of this alive. He urged his horse forward without looking back at them, but aware of their horses following behind him.

Ahead, the dark rise of the Dragoon Mountains seemed much nearer. No longer far off on the horizon, they climbed up in front of him into a great ridged barrier which held his attention for a long moment. The trail was difficult to follow under the thinning moonlight and the going was slow; however, the path ran straight for those mountains and Kendell knew where he would find those he pursued—but first he'd have to discover the secret entrance into Cochise's stronghold, and as far as he knew, no white man but the once-renowned Tom Jeffords had that knowledge.

14

If that *renegado* had followed them into the darkness, Matt Kendell was not aware of it; and for the last four hours he was making a point of being aware of everything. His nerves were set like a hair trigger and the quiet of the two youngsters following behind him was beginning to grate like an itch he couldn't quite reach to scratch. The burns pained him; he tried to dismiss them and put them out of mind, but they remained as an undercurrent to his whole mood and only added to his restlessness.

Ahead, dark land climbed while the soil beneath his animal's hooves firmed up. The rise of the Dragoon Mountains stood before him in a long, shadowed wall—much nearer now, but still a half day's ride. Kendell figured they could be into the coolness of those mountain canyons by noon if he pushed on without resting. The horizon to the east was still dark but the mountain peaks were faintly tinted a rose color as were the high bands of clouds that stretched overhead; first the clouds, then the mountaintops—in half an hour the horizon to the east would begin to show it too. Kendell reckoned the sun would be upon them in another hour, heating the land like a furnace.

As he rode along, Kendell became aware of a notion which put him ill at ease. He reined in, staring hard into the shadows. *Nerves,* he told himself as Jemima and Willie pulled up alongside. She regarded him curiously.

Willie was doing a fine job holding his own atop his wide, leggy horse. It was too tall and muscular an animal to be an Indian pony and Kendell figured it had been one of those stolen from their homestead; an animal bred in the East for drawing heavy wagons; something which had been transplanted into this desert country—something that could not last long without water. The animal would make it to those mountains all right, and there they would find water.

"Why are we stopping?" Jemima asked him evenly.

He glanced out into the darkness again as his hand tightened around the cold steel receiver of the Winchester, and looked back at the girl. "You two getting tired yet?"

"Yes, we are."

"I'm doing just fine, Mister Kendell," Willie countered quickly, but his enthusiasm did a poor job of hiding the weariness that pulled at his young face.

"Yep, I'd say you are."

"How much more are we going to have to ride?" Jemima asked.

He handed her the canteen. "Take a drink. We'll rest here a few minutes. Stretch your legs if you feel like you need it."

"I don't think I better. If I get down I'll be plain too tired to climb back up; I'll end up lying down and going to sleep."

"I could use some of that myself."

"Where *are* we going, Mister Kendell?" she asked, handing the canteen to Willie.

He nodded at the rise of land. "Into those mountains."

"But why? You haven't told us what's so important that we can't just leave this place and find a town somewhere. Pa used to say there was a place called San Pablo not too far from our home."

"I'd say my business was none of yours," he answered her, straightening up in his saddle.

Jemima's eyes narrowed. "Since you're dragging Willie and me into it, I'd say that it was our business too."

He recalled that she had also been right back at the homestead when she insisted on him cleaning his wound. For a child, Jemima possessed an uncanny ability to present an argument that left her opponent helpless to reply. He figured in another ten years she would be more woman than most men could handle—that is if he could keep her from getting killed during the next few days.

"I suppose you are right," he said, reaching for the canteen and taking a long drink before capping it and draping it over the saddle horn.

He kept the details of the San Pablo violence to a minimum. The children had seen more than enough violence and death to last them a good many years; there was no need burdening them with any more, and besides, some points were just too painful to bring up.

Jemima's face was slack when he finished. "It sounds horrible," she said.

"It was," Kendell replied, turning his horse back toward the mountains and urging it on. Jemima and Willie followed along, silent for a moment, and then she asked, "What did you do in San Pablo?"

"Do?"

"Yeah, you know, what kind of work did you do—what was your job?"

"I reckon you could say I didn't have much of a job," he

said after some thought. "At least nothing that amounted to very much work."

"But you did eat, didn't you?"

"What kind of question is that?"

"Pa always told us a man had to work if he expected to eat."

Kendell laughed. "I did eat, and I did work. I suppose you could say my job was to be around to help out when someone needed it, and they in turn gave me food and a place to live. Sort of you scratch my back and I'll scratch yours."

"Help? You mean like a hired gunfighter?"

"I reckon in some ways, but I didn't very often have need of a gun, except when I went hunting—I did a lot of hunting. Nothing revives a man's weary soul quicker than an afternoon in the field with a shotgun, a good bird dog and a bag of fresh quail."

"Pa never liked to hunt. He did it only when we needed food to eat but I don't think he ever enjoyed it. He always said he'd rather just sit in the shade of an old cottonwood tree and watch them than kill them. He said he had had enough killing during the war and intended to live out the rest of his life just as peaceful as he was able . . ." Her voice fell off. "I reckon a man can't live in peace these days even if he wants it."

"I've found it to be true that those folks who try the hardest to avoid violence usually end up with more of it than they can handle," Kendell answered her, becoming introspective. "There is a saying that the good die young. Well, I reckon the other side to that coin is the evil go on living forever."

Jemima remained thoughtfully silent.

Kendell was growing uncomfortable with the direction their conversation had taken and he said to her, "How long have you and Willie lived in Arizona?"

"Gosh, we've lived here all our lives—well, Willie has—I was just a baby when my folks came out west."

"Where did they come from?"

"Pennsylvania."

"What on God's green earth made them pick this corner of hell to settle in?"

"Our home was located in a very pleasant little valley," she retorted indignantly. "There was cool water, lots of big shady trees and plenty of grass to feed our livestock."

"I beg your pardon, ma'am. So you had a little bit of Eden tucked away in this here corner of hell. Still, there are a lot more congenial places for a man to bring his family and make a home."

She shrugged her shoulders. "They came out for my mother's health. The doctor said she needed to live in a hot, dry climate. Back in Pennsylvania she would have these spells where she couldn't breathe—she almost died once, at least that is what I am told. Well, my pa figured this was hot enough and dry enough, so he brought us out here, after spending some time looking for a place, of course. And I guess it was the right place 'cause she never did have another attack since. What about yourself, Mister Kendell, what brought you out?"

"It was as far away from my past as I could find."

"You running from the law?" she inquired with a note of surprise in her voice.

"No, nothing like that."

"Then it doesn't sound like a very good reason to me."

"I didn't realize it needed your approval," he answered her, shifting his view to the east. The horizon was wearing a halo of pink now and in another moment the sun—still below it—brought forth a rosy, predawn glow, pushing the shadows ahead of it. He directed his eyes to the mountains, still dark in the low places, and felt the hate building up again.

They were already there, he could feel it. And if he had any luck at all the trail would be readable all the way in. Then he would have his revenge!

Matt Kendell drove on, oblivious to the children behind him now. For a moment he thought of María, but he buried it as he made his plans, calculated his next moves and allowed the hate that had kept him going to flow back in.

15

Cuchillo watched the sun coming up, spreading its salmon fingers across the desert far below him. It was peaceful now—on a dawn such as this—and he could easily ignore the other horses with their anxious riders standing nearby. Mornings, before the heat arrived to stifle the life out of all living things, were always the most pleasant time of the desert. Throughout the many years of fighting this harsh land, Cuchillo had learned to stop and appreciate each new dawn, and in his own way, give thanks for it.

But the white men were different, always in a hurry—as they were now. Sargot leaned impatiently in his saddle and said, "I don't see what's so damned interesting out there that you have to waste so much time pondering on it."

Cuchillo let the words go past him. It was his mountain, his stronghold . . . now. He'd lead them on when he was good and ready. At a glance Cuchillo read their faces and only Pedro had half a heart as his for the desert, for he also was drinking in the beauty of this new dawn. Beauty was so rare on the Sonoran, one needed to take it where one found it.

Sargot moved his horse alongside Cuchillo. "I don't know for what reason you're stalling, Indian, but we had an agreement, or don't you remember that?" His hand came to rest menacingly upon the Colt at his side. "I got ways to help you remember, Indian."

Cuchillo smiled at this. "The way is before you," he said, waving an arm at the jumble of rocks, most of them twice as high as a man—a maze stretching a quarter mile in every direction. "Do you think you can find it without me?"

Sargot bit back his anger. "Why the hell do you think we brought you along?"

"Then your threat is meaningless," Cuchillo replied, glancing at the pistol.

Jones laughed and Sargot shot a wicked glance at him. He threw up his hands as if fending off the other's eyes, saying, "Hey, don't look at me; I knew right off we couldn't trust that no-good redskin."

"Well, Cuchillo?" Sargot demanded, looking back at the Indian.

Another rare smile cracked Cuchillo's lips. "I agreed to lead you to the place, and lead you I will. The trail into the canyon is steep and our horses are tired; we must rest here before starting in."

Sargot eased back at this. "I don't like just sitting around like this. As long as there might be someone coming up our trail behind us I don't much care to be wasting time."

Cuchillo looked away from him, gazing back out across the desert far below the trail they now were on. The way in was tricky—even for the devil to follow, but Cuchillo had made his preparations and now he must carry through with them. Deceit and lies were not close companions of Cuchillo but on occasion they were necessary. He said, "He no longer comes."

"What?"

"He not come anymore," Cuchillo repeated, looking into Sargot's eyes.

Sargot studied him a long moment then shook his head. "You crazy old fool! There never was anyone, was there? I knew it—I just knew you had to be lying! It was all a story you made up 'cause you had to appear wise and smart, and you wanted to keep us jumpity as rabbits. Why I ought to—!" Sargot stopped himself, aware that without Cuchillo he'd never find the hidden valley.

"Believe what you will."

"I believe you're playing some kind of game with us and I don't like it one bit!" He whipped off his hat, shaking it at the Indian, and in the early morning light his pink head looked red, as the blood of anger surged to his face. "No more games; do I make myself clear?" he said, waving the hat in a rage. "Now you turn that animal of yours around and you show us the way into that canyon, *now!*"

Deliberately slow, Cuchillo looked back to the wide desert below and gazed upon the sand turning from pink to white in the growing sunlight. Within, he knew a certain satisfaction—not so much from what he saw but more from what he now felt. He remembered standing on this very spot at Cochise's side a long time ago, watching the white soldiers approaching like a swarm of blue ants far below. He recalled the anticipation of battle which had made his blood run hot—and now he felt it again. Yes, the devil was still out there. He was still coming, and when he did, these men would have to pay . . . it made him young again just to think of it.

Cuchillo finally looked back at Sargot and nodded his ancient head. "We will go now," he said, turning his horse toward the maze of rocks.

Sargot tugged his hat back over his bald pate and moved

in behind the Indian while Jones and Pedro, leading the mule, came around behind the three women.

Jones whispered to Pedro, "Now I surely did enjoy seeing Sargot get put in his place by that Injun. Yep, he needed to be taken down a notch, don't you think?"

Pedro looked past the women to the bearded man and replied, "If you have any brains at all you won't let him know you enjoyed it."

"Bah! Sargot ain't nothin' but hot air; just a lot of wind, that's all."

Pedro grinned. He turned a dark eye upon Jones. "Wind?" he repeated skeptically. He scratched the back of his neck and said, "I suppose so, but then ain't that all a tornado is when it comes right down to it, heh? Just a lot of wind."

The smile faded from Jones' lips and his face turned sour.

As they started ahead, Juana's horse brushed near to Olinda and she whispered, "Did you hear? A rescue is not coming after all. I tell you, it *is* up to us to try an escape, or stay and die slowly at the hands of these swines."

Olinda nodded her head and the long, knotted hair hung limp around her shoulders. "You are correct, of course," she answered in a low voice, so as not to attract the attention of the men close behind her. "Do not worry, Juana; when the time comes I will do my part." She looked briefly at Ben Jones, thankful he did not notice her gaze. A cold shiver of needles went up her spine. Looking back at Juana, she said, "I will do it; you needn't worry."

Teresa moved up and her voice was low and urgent. "You are being watched."

Juana turned her head and Pedro said, "You three quit

that palavering, hear? This ain't no quilting bee; you ain't got nothing to talk about so turn around and ride."

Sargot heard this and swiveled in his saddle, saying to the girls, "Move into a line and be quick about it. Jones, the next time they bunch up like that shoot one of them."

A smile flashed across Jones' lips, lifting his spirits from their sour depths. "Right," he said, grinning at Pedro.

Pedro looked away in displeasure. Women were like other lovely things in the desert; very special indeed; he didn't much care to waste them like that.

Cuchillo found the trail with little effort; a narrow, winding path that twisted among wind-carved boulders, ancient and creased, like the lines of time that carved his own face. It was a confusing few minutes as they turned a dozen different directions wandering deeper into the rocky labyrinth, and then suddenly the trail straightened out, dropping into a steep and narrow canyon.

It was an easily defended place and Cuchillo recalled the warriors who used to hide high among the crevices guarding this entrance to the stronghold. In his mind he saw them all standing proud among the rocks. Familiar faces of friends long gone . . . dead, or worse, living on the white man's reservation. Only a few such as himself remained free, and most were old. Those who were young, who were mere children when Cochise surrendered to the white general, Howard, in 1872, had turned to raiding and killing. Someday they too would be hunted down and killed.

It grieved his heart to think of it, but that was the natural order of things for the conquered.

But here, moving slowly toward the stronghold, Cuchillo felt safe and secure despite the three armed and angry men behind him. The creases of this land were as familiar as the creases on the back of his nut-brown hands. He knew each one intimately; at any time he could disappear around a bend and melt into the rock and stone like a ghost, vanishing up a hidden canyon or down some shadowed declivity. There were many along the way and Cuchillo knew them all. He was coming home, and if he were to die now it would be a welcome end to a full life.

Matt Kendell paused to study the rising land ahead of him. The trail beneath him was vague at best and in places, where bedrock lay exposed, completely absent. What was there, however, pointed a direction and if he kept his horse's nose headed that way, he was confident he'd pick it up again.

"Are we lost, Mister Kendell?"

"No, I don't think so," he answered her with eyes turned down to the hard earth. Gazing up at the rocky slope, he said, "They appear to have headed off in that direction."

"How far ahead of us do you think they are?"

"Not very far. Judging from the way those patches of grass are trampled I'd say we're maybe four or five hours behind them."

"I'm getting a little scared."

"You'd be a fool if you weren't," he said, looking at the girl. Apparently she had forgiven him for his heavy-handedness the night before, and for some unexplainable reason he was glad. Well, it beats the silent treatment, he told himself, handing her the canteen. "Here, take a drink." He turned to the boy. "How are you doing, partner?"

"I'm all right, sir."

Kendell nodded at a canyon ahead. "We will most likely find water in there, and relief from this sun too. Once we get into that canyon we better keep our eyes and ears open. I don't think they will bother to string watches behind them because I'm figuring they won't be expecting anyone to be following them, but we need to be careful just the same." As he spoke he carefully surveyed the land about them. It was a rugged place; a place the Apaches had once considered their own. A land where a bend in the trail could put you in the middle of an Indian ambush, and he figured a hundred Indians could hide up in those rocks and he would never know it.

Well, as far as he knew, the Indians were all gone—most of them, that is. But that was no guarantee they were all alone here, on this trail leading up into the Dragoon Mountains. He recalled Annie's dying words: *As long as that one is alive, he'll have but one thing in his head and that will be to kill you.*

She was a crazy old woman but he figured her dying words were not something to be taken lightly. A man who ignores warning is a man liable to step down on a rattlesnake someday, he told himself, remembering that feeling of someone nearby which he had had earlier that morning while still in the darkness. It may have been only the racing of his blood as he neared his goal—it could have been nothing but nerves, as he had suspected at the time. Just the same, it had been a real feeling, and even now, thinking back on it, his fist wrapped instinctively around the rifle in his hand until his knuckles turned white. He made a conscious effort to open his fingers and drew in a deep breath, releasing it slowly and allowing the tension to drain away.

"You two ready to move on?" he asked.

"I guess so," Jemima said and Willie handed the canteen back to him.

The trail soon petered out but once beneath the canyon walls, where vegetation and soft earth lay protected from the burning sun, Kendell began to pick up snatches of it again. Ironclad hooves had trampled the vegetation here. A stream trickled down, they had paused to water their horses. Kendell did the same, filling up the canteens before moving on.

Farther up, the canyon branched. Kendell reined to a stop. The rocky floor showed no signs as to which way they had gone and either way appeared as uninviting as the other. He studied the two arms of the canyon a long time, drawing a blank. Then something caught his eye. From a crevice up the rocky wall above his head a small plant was growing. It was beyond what normally would have been affected by the passage of animals and riders, yet the stem of it was snapped to one side, pointing up the right-hand branch of the canyon, as if someone had reached up while riding past and twisted it as a sign.

A sign?

Kendell's brow wrinkled. It could mean but three things. Either they were leaving a trail for friends to follow later, or they knew he was coming for them and they were trying to throw him off their trail—which he didn't believe as it would be just too easy to bushwhack him and be done with it—or, lastly, someone was deliberately laying down a trail for him to follow—but who? One of the girls?

It puzzled him. It could be nothing at all—the careless act of a bored rider stretching in his saddle—but whatever the reason for it, it brought the hairs on his neck straight and his eyes roamed cautiously along the dark canyon walls before moving ahead.

But the darkness held no dangers and in a little while the trail became clear again in the soft earth down by the water's edge. An hour later their horses scrambled up a steep embankment and out of the canyon, into the open where the sun glared white-hot off the burning rocks. The trail remained steep, climbing higher into the Dragoon Mountains, and several hours later Kendell came suddenly to a stop. The trail they had been following vanished into a jumbled maze of etched boulders strewn across the landscape as far as he could see. As if a gaint hand had scooped them up and tossed them out as a child might toss out a handful of jacks.

Kendell studied the fantastic formations and recalled the stories he had heard of the entrance to Cochise's stronghold. So this is what it really looked like. A man could be lost for weeks in this frantic land, the storytellers had told him, and now with despair creeping into his heart, Matt Kendell understood why.

16

Buffered by towering cliffs, its fire dissipated on the glaring rocks high above, the devil sun was a gentler beast now as its easy light filtered down on the riders. It was cool between the canyon walls and in single file their horses struggled with the steep trail.

Sargot's eyes remained intense, burning down upon Cuchillo's back. He did not like following the old Chiricahua Apache down this forbidden trail, he did not like being dependent on the Indian to take him to this place of refuge, where they would hide until the furor over what they had done back in San Pablo had died down and they could continue on in safety to Mexico. Any trust he might have placed in Cuchillo was gone and for a time he harbored a notion to be rid of the savage here and now. His hand came to rest on his pistol, but as with each previous time Sargot restrained himself. Perhaps he could find the stronghold alone, now that they were in the final chute—he was certain the end of this canyon would open up on the place he wanted to be—but perhaps there was still a trick or two left in this passage. Another couple of hours would make little difference now, and besides, there was still a treasure or two to be found up ahead with Cuchillo's help.

Cuchillo continued on without a backward glance. His shoulders remained relaxed and he was careful each time that feeling came over him not to tighten and hunch them forward, as a man expecting an attack from that direction might. He was an old man now, and he didn't get that way by ignoring those feelings, but he knew whatever was to happen to him would happen ahead, in the valley, not here, not at this moment.

The hours passed in silence but for the scraping of iron against rock and the snorting of their animals. Then all at once the passage made a bend and spilled out onto a wide green valley encircled by steep walls too straight and smooth for a man to climb.

"Well, I'll be damned," Sargot said, kicking his horse into a gallop and riding out into the center of the valley. Jones and Pedro, with the mule and the three prisoners, joined him, and their horses tugged at the tall green grass.

Cuchillo hesitated by the break, allowing his eyes to roam across the valley. His eyes saw not the wide grassy bowl of the valley, or the pool of clear water bubbling from the spring—or the white men who now desecrated *his* valley. Instead he saw the valley as it had been twenty years earlier. Where rings of blackened stones rested in the depths of the tall grass, Cuchillo saw campfires and smelled wood smoke. Where low mounds of twisted sticks lay across the ground, gray with age, half buried and rotted, Cuchillo saw stands of wickiups, friends relaxing in safety and playing games. The laughter of little children sounded in his ear, and the clicking of stones as the women sat together grinding grain for bread.

It was good to be home.

Cuchillo rode out into the valley like a man searching for something. He stopped and looked at the cliffs above. What he sought, he located at once high up the gray wall; a rock in the shape of a hawk. He was not fully aware of the smile which came to his lips as he began searching the ground. In another moment he swung out of his saddle, feeling the soft grass beneath his moccasins, and knelt down above a pile of stiff buffalo hides, rotting for a score of years under the silent sun. They were his, and he recalled the hours he had spent preparing them, stretching then stacking them carefully to wait upon the day of his return, which never came —until now.

A spray of decaying lodgepoles formed a circle in the grass nearby. Grass clutched them to the earth—the mother of all things—and Cuchillo walked amongst them, finding a place where his spirit was at ease—and there he sat down. Here, through the door of his wickiup he used to watch the stone hawk forever soaring upon the valley wall. Of all the things this place had been, only the hawk remained unchanged.

To his left, buried beneath years of sod and spreading weeds were the stones, still black from cook fires. As he studied them now he became aware of the spirit of Sun Rising kneeling beside the fire, grinding maize in her mortar. She paused, looked across to Cuchillo and smiled. When he blinked the vision was gone; he brushed at a spot of moisture which had gathered in the corner of his eye. It was not good to show tears and he looked away, allowing the past to fall silent, seeing the valley for what it was: clean, fresh, lonely and—his black eyes hardened turning to the white men—desecrated.

Cuchillo drew a long breath. The stone hawk was all that remained of the past. Then an old memory made him turn to examine the valley wall far to his right. There, folded into the shadows was a declivity. A fissure never touched by sunlight and all but impossible to find if someone were to look for it. The passage was narrow, through a small cave, and opened onto another valley less than an acre wide. His eyes fixed on that sliver of darkness and in his mind he saw the burial procession with the pallet borne upon their shoulders. Sun Rising had been as lovely in death as she was in life—his loving wife who had died giving him a son, and then took the boy with her. The infant together with his mother—forever.

The past was alive all around him and Cuchillo turned his eyes away from that shadowed valley wall determined to tread those sacred burial grounds at least one more time before leaving this place.

But now it was a dangerous thing to dwell too long among the ashes of the past. Danger was nearing and it would require all of his cunning if he was ever to leave this valley alive. Death held no sting for the old man, he had lived a long, full life, yet he was in no great hurry to cross over into that great unknown. He stood up and gathered the reins of his grazing horse, then started for the group in the center of his valley.

"The Indian is coming," Pedro said, quickly glancing to the ground as though there was something there to attract his attention, but out of the corner of his eyes he was keeping tabs on Cuchillo.

"What do you think that old Injun was up to anyway?"

Sargot said to Jones, "How the hell do I know? That crazy old man might be up to anything and I'll tell you this, I don't trust him. The sooner I'm rid of him, the better I'll like it."

"I can take care of it right now," Jones said, easing the gun from his holster.

"No, put it away. I still need him around a while longer."

"For what?"

"He knows where Cochise is buried, that's what for."

Jones snorted. "Who the hell cares? Cochise ain't nothin' but a pile of dried-up bones by this time, if there's even that much left of him."

Sargot sneaked a glance over his shoulder and said hurriedly, "Listen, when these Indians bury a chief, they bury them with their forty-year's gatherin's. That means most everything Cochise owned will be buried there with him. Hell, that man has become something of a legend; if we can find his body and take some of his personal belongin's back with us they'd be worth their weight in gold."

Pedro nodded his head in agreement. "It is true, some people will pay a fancy price for Cochise's war-lance or his headdress."

"You guys have gone loco. I ain't agonna go diggin' up no dead Injun! That mule is totin' all the gold I care about."

"You don't dig up Indians!" Sargot hissed. "They don't bury them in the ground, they put up poles and lay the bodies on pallets eight or ten feet up. All's we got to do is kick down one of them poles and Cochise will practically fall into our laps."

Jones' mouth puckered in as if he'd just taken a bite from a sour pickle. "Just fall in our laps?" he said with some disgust. "Why the hell don't they plant 'em like normal folks?"

Sargot shrugged his shoulders. "I reckon on occasion they do, but mostly they hoist the body off the ground so as their soul don't have no trouble in escaping to the sky—least that's the way I heard it."

"Sounds like somethin' an Injun might do."

"Quiet down; here he comes," Pedro warned.

Sargot said in a loud voice, "I reckon we need to set up a camp now." He turned, feigning surprise at seeing Cuchillo, and said, "Oh there you are. I was beginning to wonder where you got off to."

Cuchillo's dark eyes saw past the bearded man's deceptive smile. Then his eyes turned up to the blue sky, attracted by the ebony flicker of a pair of ravens circling lazily overhead on the warm air, wings stretched flat out—a crow soars with wingtips reaching upward, for the sun, and at a distance that distinction was the only way to tell the two birds apart. The raven knows when a man's heart is evil and now they were coming to warn Cuchillo—but their warning was unnecessary for the old man already knew this about Sargot.

"You done good by us, leading us to this place, Cuchillo."

"It is a place that holds many memories," he replied.

"I'll just bet it does, Cochise," Jones said.

Cuchillo turned slowly toward him, his hand upon the hilt of his belt knife, then he shifted his eyes away from the man's skinny face, staring past it. Suddenly, Cuchillo was grinning.

"Hey, what you up to, old man?" he said, jerking his head over his shoulder, then looking back at Cuchillo. But the Indian was still staring out into empty space.

"I asked you a question, damn it!"

"You spoke his name, now he wants to know what the white man wants of him."

"What? Who wants to know?"

"Cochise wants to know."

"That man is dead—you crazy Injun!"

"You summoned him by speaking his name in this place. His spirit roams this valley and now it has come. It stands by your side."

Jones' eyeballs rolled back and forth as his hand drew out the pistol at his side.

"A gun is no threat to a spirit," Cuchillo said.

Sargot laughed. "He got you spooked real good this time, Jones."

"Shut up!" Jones said, shoving the pistol back into its holster, and Sargot laughed all the harder. He turned on Cuchillo. "The next time you play one of your crazy jokes on me you're a dead man. Do you hear me, Indian?"

Cuchillo's eyes narrowed and looked up at the pair of ravens overhead. "Do you see them?" he asked. "They come from the world beyond; they come to take a spirit home with them." He paused, considering Jones for a moment. "They have eyes that can see into a man's heart—I think they are looking into your heart now."

Jones' mouth screwed into a knot. "I don't have to stand here listening to your stupid superstitions," he said, and he stomped away, pausing after a dozen paces to look quickly around himself. Heaving his narrow shoulders, he turned back to them, saying, "I'll start gathering some firewood, Jake; where you want to set up camp?"

"It don't matter to me; you pick the spot, anyplace you feel comfortable in, only you best make certain there ain't no Indian spirits fixing to use the same campsite, heh?"

Infuriation brought a shudder to his pencil-thin frame and Ben Jones turned his back on them in a rage.

"He'll get over it," Pedro said, mildly amused.

"Get over it? What makes you think I'm in any hurry for him to calm down—he can stew from now till hell freezes over for all the sweat I'll give over his pouting."

Cuchillo went to the women and helped them out of their saddles. Sargot nodded his head at the old Indian and said to Pedro, "Go on and give the old man a hand."

"Sure thing."

Juana was not accustomed to spending so much time upon the back of a horse, and now the weary hours of riding, the sleepless nights, the exhausting torment of fulfilling Sargot's lusty needs were taking their toll on her and she sat wearily down upon the grass.

"Are you all right?" Olinda asked, sitting down beside her.

"I am just so tired, I cannot go on any farther."

Teresa stood above the two of them, and remained standing, straight and proud. She would never allow the men to see her break under their torment. She said, "We will be able to rest here and regain our strength. I have a feeling this is as far as they intend to take us, and that we will never leave this place alive."

Olinda's dark eyes grew large. "Do not say such a thing; where there is life there is still hope."

Teresa laughed. "Yes, we have the hope of Juana's plan and, I agree, it is our only hope, but it is hope dangling from a little thread called luck; and it is a very fine thread indeed."

"But you do believe that the plan will be successful—don't you?" Olinda asked.

"We do not need dissension among ourselves," Juana said sharply. "What we must do is difficult enough without sowing more seeds of doubt, Teresa."

Teresa lifted her head. Sargot and Pedro were standing by the horses, Cuchillo had moved some distance away and was staring out across the pool of shining water. "Whether or not it will work makes little difference now. The fact that it is our only possible chance of escape is what is important, and I would rather die while trying than not to try at all—and die just the same."

"You will not die, Teresa, you are too strong." Juana laid back on the grass and folded an arm across her eyes. "If anyone must die, it will be me."

"No one must die!" Olinda said. "We must not think this way."

"You are right, Olinda, and I am sorry. We must nurture our hope. If we begin to think we are defeated, we surely will be defeated. Well, I for one am going to make the best of this; I feel filthy and there is plenty of fresh water here. I can see no reason why I should not be able to wash myself." Gazing down at Olinda and Juana, she added, "You will feel better too if you do the same." Teresa went to Sargot and thrust out her bound hands.

"I need to wash and there is no place here that we can run off to."

He considered her request and untied her hands. "You can go and untie your friends too, but the three of you better mind yourselves. If you even give me a notion you're up to something, I'll kill the lot of you. That'll be a whole lot easier than watching my backside."

"What danger could three women be to a man like you?"

Sargot grinned, knowing her words were true. "You just remember what I told you."

"I will," Teresa said, rubbing her sore wrists. "We will give you no trouble."

She returned to her friends and untied their hands. Together, they walked down to the water's edge and washed the desert from their arms and faces.

17

After a while one rock began to look like another to Matt Kendell, and when the shadows started gathering in the low places, filling in the spaces between them, he decided it was time to stop and reconnoiter the situation. He stood up in the stirrups, looking around.

It was difficult to keep track of the hours while winding through the shifting light of those towering boulders because his eyes were turned down to study the ground for signs of the passage of riders; it was easy to lose half a day in the effort. Pulling up, Kendell figured it was late afternoon and he had wasted most of it riding circles and following false leads. He had never been very good at tracking in his youth and he cursed the years of easy living which had taken the edge off of any expertise in that art which he might have once possessed. Yet he had to keep trying. To have come this far only to be turned back in the end by a rock puzzle—it was a notion he would not entertain.

"Another dead end?" Jemima asked and there was genuine disappointment in her voice. Finding the secret entrance into Cochise's stronghold was becoming something of an obsession with the three of them; the fear Jemima experienced earlier was being replaced with determination.

He turned his horse around. "We'll start over again; one of these trails has to lead us to where we want to go."

"Are you sure?"

"Their tracks lead into this maze, and they're not here now so they must have gotten through it somewhere . . . yeah, I'm sure."

"You know it is getting late?"

"Yeah, I know."

"Aren't you getting hungry?"

It hadn't occurred to him, but now that she mentioned it Kendell realized his stomach had been trying to tell him that same thing, only he was too caught up in what he was up to to pay it any mind.

"I reckon I am, now that you mention it. I reckon you two could use something to eat, too."

"Yes, sir."

"All I have is some jerky."

"That sounds just fine to me, Mister Kendell," Willie chimed in.

Kendell looked at the boy narrowly. "Well, I reckon you must be just plain starving to say a thing like that. Come on, let's find our way out of this puzzle, boil us some coffee water and take a breather."

When they dismounted Jemima and Willie scampered off to collect twigs for a fire. Kendell loosened the cinches and led the animals to a place where solitary tufts of grass grew along the base of the rocks. For a moment he was all alone; the children gathering wood and chattering were the only sounds riding the high and lonely wind. Looking out across the desert that stretched in every direction below him, he again felt akin with the hard and deadly land. Staring out, a vision of the smoking ruins of San Pablo momentarily occupied his brain; this time he allowed it to pass without much effort. Something was different. Unlike the relentless desert below him, he was changing. Where had all the hate gone, he wondered, and without fully realizing it his eyes turned toward the two children, playfully filling their arms with firewood.

A movement in the shadows caught the corner of his eye and he swung toward it, pulling the gun from his waistband as he moved. Now nothing stirred and his eyes leaped from one shadowed place to another. He stalked around the boulder, melting into the darkness on the other side, and, as he suspected, no one was there. Before returning, he checked around, turning up nothing. A long breath helped the tension drain away and he decided this was a kind of place where even the bravest of men might visualize danger lurking in the shadows.

The children were waiting for him when he returned. "Where were you, Mister Kendell?"

"Just looking around, Willie."

"Oh."

They built up a fire and by the time their stomachs stopped groaning, satisfied by the meager fare, and the coffee had boiled, the sunlight was gone and darkness had settled across the land. There would be no finding the secret entrance tonight, and with that somber thought they made themselves comfortable.

Willie and Jemima were soon asleep by the fire while Kendell sat in the silence of the night, listening to the wind, his ears straining for a noise which never came. As the fire died down he pulled a blanket over the two of them and arranged another by his saddle, placing his hat on the saddle where his head should have been then moving some distance away. He found a place beside a rock where he had a clear view of the campsite, and the kids, and settled in.

A slice of hard jerky washed down with a sip of cold coffee; that was how this night was going to go—and the way he saw it, it was going to be a long one. The night was already cool and he hunched into himself to try to keep warm and wait it out.

Sargot wiped his greasy fingers on his shirt, then dragged a sleeve across his mouth. "Chicken!" he said, chewing, "damn, who'd expect we find chickens running around in this place."

"We brought many chickens here, and the white man's cows—those we could steal and bring across the desert without their dying from the dryness. There are fish in the pond and enough rabbits to feed many men. Cochise's braves never wanted for food here. In the desert every day was a game of survival, but here we rested and lived well."

"This is a right pleasant place you got here, Cuchillo; yep, a man could get right comfortable," Sargot said.

"I'd just a soon be somewheres else," Jones said irritably.

Pedro chuckled. "Don't tell me you're still bothered by Cochise."

Jones tensed. "You don't get off my back about that you'll be picking knuckles from your teeth."

"I rather doubt that," Pedro replied in an even voice.

"If you two are gonna fight, take it somewhere else. I'm in no mood for it now."

"Hell, we ain't gonna fight, Jake, we're just funning with each other—ain't that right, Ben?"

The skinny man sneered into his coffee. Pedro leaned

back against his saddle, laughing quietly to himself, and Sargot turned his stare from them to Cuchillo.

"Tell me about this place," he said.

"What can one tell of it?"

"You spent a lot of time here, didn't you?"

Cuchillo nodded his head. "For many years this valley was the home of my people."

Sargot spent a moment gazing into the fire, then said, "I heard tell that Cochise is buried somewhere around here. Is that true?"

"Many Apaches are buried here."

"Where? I haven't seen anything that looks like an Indian burial ground."

"Is the burial place of my people a concern of yours?"

Sargot watched the glowing coals fanned by the wind, listening to the crackle of the fire. "You don't have to tell me nothin', Cuchillo, I was just curious, that's all."

"I agreed to lead you to this valley because you said you needed a safe place to wait, and I needed to see my home once more before I died; we each had something to gain. This I did. But I will not show you the sacred burial place of my chief."

"It ain't important, Cuchillo, I was just curious, that's all, but I know how you people feel about the dead so just forget I even asked."

He grew uncomfortable under Cuchillo's dark stare, wondering how much the Indian knew of his intentions, debating whether he should pull his gun and kill the old man now or wait. He tugged a leg off a roasting chicken and said, "Yep, never in the world expected to catch us chicken for dinner."

"They need food, too," Cuchillo said, lifting the remains of the chickens from the fire and rising to take them to the three woman huddled together beyond the ring of firelight.

Sargot eased back as the Indian's gaze left him. "Yeah, give 'em something to eat," he said, "and take 'em some water, too. Got to keep their strength up 'cause I got plans for one of 'em after I'm finished here." Sargot laughed and went back to gnawing on a chicken bone.

Cuchillo gathered together the food and canteen and brought it to them. Their low talking stopped as he hunched down beside them.

"There is not much left, but a little is better than nothing."

"Thank you," Olinda said.

Cuchillo handed her the meat and set the canteen on the ground between them. Glancing back at Sargot, he continued in a guarded voice.

"That one will come for you tonight."

Juana was aware that it was her Cuchillo was speaking to. She turned her head up at him. "It does not surprise me." It was a chore to make her voice sound indifferent. Olinda had stiffened at Cuchillo's words and now her eyes stared hard at Juana.

They all knew eventually the time would come, and they knew the things they had to do when it did, but inside—in their hearts, none of them was anxious to face it. Too many variables were involved, too many emotions, too many questions; not the least of them the nagging doubt each one secretly nursed—once the action started would they be able to see it through to the end? Not a one of them had ever killed an animal, let alone a man and until you actually pull the trigger or thrust the knife, you really don't know if you are capable of it.

Of the three, Olinda harbored the greatest doubts, her face was rigid as if its lines had been carved upon the face of a marble bust.

Juana glanced quickly away from her, fearing the look upon Olinda's face was about to reveal their treachery. Cuchillo's silent presence on this journey had made her fear him—he saw much more than he let on, his ears seemed to hear what others could not; what was he seeing now in Olinda's frightened eyes, what had he overheard that night when they first formulated their plan? Perhaps even now their deception was known and all hope was indeed gone.

"What are you looking at?" Juana demanded, feeling his eyes penetrating her soul.

Cuchillo's gray head shook slowly. "You are about to fight a worthy battle," he said in a low voice while his eyes remained fixed on hers. "It is a battle which you may win, but I think not . . . not if you fight it tonight."

His words petrified her. *He knows!* She struggled with panic, then Cuchillo reached out a consoling hand, resting it upon her taut shoulder.

"Do not fear me, little one, it is not this Apache, but they you must fear. Listen to me," and his eyes roamed to the break in the valley wall where the canyon entranceway cut back. "Tomorrow, when the sun is up in the east, wait until then."

"What . . . what are you talking about?" Juana stammered, grasping at whatever veil of secrecy was left of their scheme. But her heart told her this man already knew it all.

He merely smiled at her, stood and disappeared into the shadows.

"Oh, what does he mean?" Olinda asked after Cuchillo had melted quietly into the darkness of the valley. Juana remained unmoved, her frightened eyes staring at the place where he had disappeared.

"He knows what we are up to," Teresa said. "He must have overheard—"

"But what will that mean for us?" she repeated with a note of urgency edging her voice.

Teresa shook her head. "I don't know."

Juana glanced back at the girls; both of them looking to her for guidance now—well, it had been her idea; she would have to take the responsibility for their next step.

Tomorrow, when the sun is up in the east, wait until then.

What was he trying to tell her? Did he know her plans so intimately as to even know at that very instant the thoughts in her head? How could she trust him? How could she trust anyone who was involved in the horror of San Pablo? With the suddenness of a spring rain, Juana was drenched in confusion where only a moment before her mind was firmly set upon what had to be done next.

"Juana?" Olinda prodded.

"I'm thinking!" she shot back with a violent jerk of her head.

"You had better think faster," Teresa commented; the strain in her voice told Juana she was working hard at not being obviously anxious. "One of the pigs has just left his sty and I believe he is coming your way, Juana."

"All right . . . all right, listen to me. I do not know if we can trust that Indian or not, but if he is being truthful with us, and he does know something we don't, well . . . well I guess it won't hurt anything if we wait until the morning—if that will mean the difference between success and failure."

"Yes, we should wait," Olinda added quickly, and then he was standing over them.

Jake Sargot towered above the three women, not speaking a word, studying them as one might study a thing which had just crawled out from beneath a rock. His view shifted to Juana and a smile twisted his lips.

"Come on," he said, snatching her up by the wrist, "let's take a walk."

She whimpered at the pain of his grasp, stumbling after him into the darkness.

18

Even in the blackness of night the trail was plain to Cuchillo. Midnight or noon, it made no difference to the old man. His feet had eyes which needed no light to see by, and now they traveled a path which, sadly, they had traveled many times before.

He paused to look back. The small enclosure of the valley was dark but for the point of light flickering bloodred in the distance. At that moment someone stood and moved, casting a shadow which obscured the firelight for an instant, then the red glow of the embers was again visible.

The moon overhead was a thin sliver of a crescent adding little light to the valley, and that was just fine for Cuchillo's purposes; he'd as soon give up his life here and now, as to lead those three into the sacred place. Looking back at their camp, he knew it was safe to continue on. It would be many hours before they would begin to miss him considering what was currently occupying their time.

At a place along the valley wall, the mountain junipers grew thick, almost choking each other. This was the place. Cuchillo slipped among the trees on a trail that would be all but invisible even in the light of day, and felt the narrow path rising beneath his feet. After skirting the vertical wall several paces he paused to draw in a breath of mountain air and study the dark valley floor. Although not obvious now that night obscured the land around him, Cuchillo knew he had climbed several dozen feet; the campfire in the middle of the valley appeared to rest at a slightly different angle from the last time he had viewed it.

A coyote sang a lonely song from the walls high over Cuchillo's head. It was answered from across the valley, and then another yelped. Alone where none could see it, Cuchillo allowed a smile to spread freely across his face.

The trail that he followed, climbing the valley wall, was a thin thread of rock made for mountain goats, surefooted burros—and men, too. When it made a sharp turn, what little light had been there was suddenly gone. It did not matter. He knew the way precisely, recognizing even the slightest irregularities of the rocky path beneath his moccasins. The air was musty here and Cuchillo recalled the little pool which used to lie ahead, formed from a trickle of water dripping through a crack in the ceiling of the cavern. All at once his moccasins splashed into it and he proceeded with more caution, remembering that slippery green slime covered the shallow basin. The darkness before him faded to gray and shortly he was standing in the open once again.

Peering ahead, he felt a lump in his throat. They were all here, in this small place, his friends, his loved ones, raised to the sky upon ashen skeletons of thin poles. The uneven land beneath them was but a foundation for the burial tiers that spread like a forest inside the confining walls.

Cuchillo fell to his knees, removing the medicine bag from around his neck. In the quiet of the night he raised his voice in a low, almost imperceptible chant. He announced to the spirits who he was and why he had come and then a warm glow of peace settled inside him. They had accepted him. Cuchillo rose to his feet and walked into the burial ground.

19

The night had grown quiet, too quiet for Matt Kendell's liking. Back in the shadows, where he sat hidden among the rocks, he was aware of his shoulders tightening under the cloth of his shirt and knew there was no good reason for it that he could tell—except that something was now tugging at his subconscious, something he knew should not be ignored.

The fire in the clearing had died down. In the thin moonlight the dark shapes of Jemima and Willie curled under the blanket, alongside the bedroll he'd fixed up to look like a third sleeping body, blended in with the darkness of the ground. The bedroll had been an afterthought; whether or not it would fool anyone was debatable; it was, however, all he had had to work with at the time.

All at once Kendell sat bolt upright. Had something moved out there, beyond where the children were sleeping? His gun was in his hand while he strained to see, or hear, what it was that had disturbed him. In another moment the questioning returned—ever since old Annie's threats he had been seeing movement where there was none; now he had gone most of the night without sleep because of the fears her words had placed in his head—or were they justified?

Throwing the blanket off his shoulders, he skirted the edge of the nearby boulder. The clearing beyond was quiet and Kendell stood listening to his own breathing, feeling the hairs rising off the nape of his neck. His night-accustomed eyes probed all the places which might hide a man and saw nothing.

Yet something nettled him now.

Turning to his right, a blurred shape suddenly leaped out at him, struck his back and tugged something hard and stiff around his throat.

Kendell tumbled forward digging his fingers into the leather belt being twisted around his neck and pulling on it sharply so that the Indian rolled out into the clearing, leaping instantly to his feet.

Kendell tore the holster belt from around his neck and was up again a moment before the shining blade of the Indian's knife flashed out. He hopped back, avoiding the steel edge, and his eyes darted away, searching for the pistol which had been knocked out of his hand.

Then the Indian was on him and they rolled across the clearing onto the dead campfire and back again, Kendell holding the savage's knife hand away from him. The Indian's face and his black eyes fierce with passion and hate—well, he'd become intimately familiar with both those emotions this past week—were inches from his own and Kendell tried to ignore those eyes, concentrating instead on the blade hovering above his head. He twisted out from under it, rolling the Indian off him and coming over on top.

In the shuffling of positions the blade moved off its mark, giving Kendell an opening. He threw a short jab and a trickle of blood creased the Indian's mouth, a second blow stunned him for an instant; long enough for Kendell to get a good grip on the knife hand, but the Indian recovered instantly, putting everything he had into the struggle.

A knee jab into the side sent Kendell rearing backward with pain. The old wound opened up again. The Indian reared up like a cornered wolverine and struck out, throwing Kendell off him. He lashed out with the blade. Kendell knocked away the first blow, getting hold of the knife again.

A rifle shot split the night; Jemima was shouting something he could not make out. The Indian's face turned up just in time to see the butt of the Henry rifle clubbing down. Jemima wasn't taking any chances when she swung it and the Indian went out like a puff on a candle, the momentum of the swing pulling her down too. She sat there a moment, a little stunned, trying to work the lever on the rifle.

Standing unsteadily, Kendell took the rifle from her and leaned up against a rock to catch his breath. Jemima stared with fright at the Indian, all at once aware of what she had done. She had been awakened suddenly, startled by the fight, and without a second thought grabbed the rifle and fired it in the air. Then she took the next logical and immediate step, short of shooting at the Indian and possibly hitting Kendell too, and just clobbered the hell out of him. Nice going, little one, he thought.

"Thanks," he said after getting his breathing down to somewhere near normal.

"Are you all right?" she asked him.

Blood was running through his fingers and the stain on the shirt growing. He winced and said, "It isn't ever going to heal if I don't quit breaking it open like this."

"It wasn't your fault," she said, dead serious.

He grinned at her. "I was just kidding."

"But how can you joke at a time like this?"

It was a good question and he didn't know the answer.

"I'll be just fine," he told her. "We better get this fellow tied up before he comes to. You swing one heck of a rifle."

"I . . . I guess I didn't even think about it. I just did it."

"That's the way you get things done. If you had taken the time to think on it first, you might never have taken action, and the way it was going, I'd probably be dead by now, and you and Willie, too."

"Do you think I hurt him?"

"I certainly hope you did."

"I don't . . . at least not too badly. He is one of them, isn't he? One of the Indians that was with that old lady."

"Yep. The fish that got away."

"And he followed us all the way here."

"Uh-huh."

"But why should he? You think he really believed he had to kill you because you killed Annie?"

"That would be part of it, but there was something else, something called vengeance. It'll drive a man to do most anything. It can make a man crazy—even crazier than that old lady."

Jemima hesitated, then said, "Like it's makin' you crazy, Mister Kendell?"

Well, it was true, wasn't it? No denying he had been acting a little on the crazy side, and now he suddenly felt exposed in front of her. Had it been that obvious that even a child could see it? Or was Jemima a special child already in command of grown-up feelings and thoughts? She certainly had an unnerving way of always being right.

Kendell said, "There is a rope on my saddle. Go get it."

When she returned, she asked, "What are we going to do with him?"

"Do? Well, first we're going to make good and sure he can't get away when he comes to. When he does regain his senses, we'll give him a drink of water and something to eat. In short, we'll put him back into as best shape as we can so he's fit for walking, since we haven't got an extra horse and it appears he followed us on foot."

"But why?"

"You see, Jemima," he said, tugging the rope tight around the Indian's wrists then starting on his feet, "this here Indian is our ticket into Cochise's stronghold."

Jemima looked at him without speaking. She didn't have to; he knew exactly what she was thinking. He was still going after them—wasn't he—crazy or not, he still had vengeance blood on his mind. Well, maybe he did, and just maybe he was crazy too, but like he had told her before, it was none of her business.

He found his gun and retrieved his holster belt, thankful to have it back again, then built a fresh fire. The night was near spent and there was no sense trying to sleep, and no good reason now why he had to wait out the dawn without some hot coffee to keep him awake.

The Indian came around a few minutes later, wrestled with the ropes he discovered on his wrists and ankles and finally, when he knew there was no escaping them, stared hard at Kendell.

"Here you go, I reckon you could use a drink of water too," he said, holding the canteen to the Indian's lips. "You speak English?"

He nodded his head.

"Good, that will make this partnership a whole lot easier and pleasant, won't it?"

From where he sat on the ground, Cuchillo turned his head upward. Above him stretched the pallet where Sun Rising and his son had once laid in death; there wasn't much left up there now but memories. Beyond the pallet the night sky arched overhead in a blue-black canopy frantic with stars—the kind of stars visible only in the clear high-mountain air; sharp and vivid, as if close enough to reach up and touch. Cuchillo fixed his stare on those heavens and then his eyes narrowed and his head turned to the south, to the valley wall rising up there, and he stared at it as if it were transparent glass . . . listening to the wind.

Like the gentle sounds of water rippling on the surface of a pond, the Devil Wind speaks. Cuchillo recalled his boyhood, sitting in the lodge of the medicine man, hearing him tell of it. It was said only a few can hear the words of the Devil Wind; words usually of warning, sometimes of death.

Then a vision appeared overhead and Cuchillo looked up to see Sun Rising drifting near to him. As he watched the spirit approach he was comforted by the smile upon her lips—the same smile he remembered she had given their newborn son as she had cradled the infant in her arms moments before death reached out its hand to claim them both. It was not pleasant to be alone in this sacred place, suddenly writhing with visions, but it was not frightening to the old man, either. Those dead in this place had loved him in life and they could mean him no harm now. There was a message here and a lesson to be learned. But now they were telling him he must leave.

He stood and the vision vanished. A tear touched the corner of his eye as suddenly he understood what it was she had tried to tell him. At the mouth of the cave Cuchillo turned back but all was silent as it had been when he first entered. It was a good place, he thought putting his back to it—a good place for the body to rest when the spirit leaves.

Emerging from the cavern upon the dark valley, his mind was occupied with other thoughts. The campfire in the distance burned brighter now than the last time he had seen it. The men would have finished with their sport and would now begin to wonder about his whereabouts. It was late and Cuchillo had no desire to spend the rest of the night in the company of white men after being in the presence of the spirits of his own people—and besides that, he knew returning to their camp would mean death for him. He would not live to see the sun of another day if he did that, and there were still many things to be done before he returned to the sacred place he had just left.

20

Jake Sargot stepped from the shadows into the ring of light cast by the campfire and squatted there, pouring himself some coffee. Pedro gazed up from where he sat against his saddle, watched him a moment, then offered him the bottle he'd been drinking from.

"Here, have some of this."

Sargot looked up, peering hard into the night at him. "What's that you got there?"

"Whiskey."

"Where the hell did you . . . ?"

"The cantina back in San Pablo. I've been saving it for a proper time."

The coffee sizzled on the hot coals as Sargot splashed out the contents of his cup and grabbed the bottle out of Pedro's hand. He took a long drink from it and said, "Damn, that's good. I ought to shoot you for not bringing this out sooner."

Pedro grinned. "If I had it would be all drunk up by now. You'd have killed yourself in the desert with that whiskey dehydrating you. Anyway, you go shooting me now and you'll never find the other bottles that I got stashed."

Jake Sargot laughed and took another swig. "A man like you could be handy to keep around, Pedro," he said.

"I was hoping you'd feel that way, Jake," he answered, snatching the bottle from Sargot.

Their heads turned at the sound of approaching footsteps

and Jones appeared out of the darkness, stopped, shook his head and said to Sargot, "I went clear around to the other side of the pond and there ain't no sign of him nowhere." He paused, sniffing the air, and said, "Hey, what's that? You guys smell somethin'?"

"What you smelling, Jones?" Sargot said straight-facedly.

He sniffed again. "I dunno. Smells like whiskey."

"You're dreaming, Jones."

"No, Jake, I smell it—I truly do."

Pedro grinned at the two of them, tipped up the bottle and let the whiskey burn his throat. Jones' eyes flared and he said, "It is whiskey! Where the Devil . . . here, give it to me!"

Pedro handed over the bottle and Sargot said, "Better treat him right or he ain't gonna tell us where he hid the rest of it."

"You got more?"

"Two more bottles."

"Hot damn! I know where I'm agonna be spending the rest of this here night. Right here with good ole Pedro."

"Not until we find that Indian."

"Told you, Jake, I went clear round to the other side of this here damned valley—and I didn't much care for it, neither, tramping around out there in the dark."

"Run into any friendly ghosts, heh?"

Jones shot a hard glance at Pedro. "Don't you go starting in on me again."

"Hey, just joking. Don't get yourself all worked up to doing something both you and I will regret; I'm the one with the whiskey, remember?"

Jones eased back and then grinned at him. "Hell, you're

right; I reckon it is bad manners to go and kill the local barkeep anyway, ain't it?"

"I think so," Pedro replied.

Sargot said, "We keep on looking. I don't like it with him out there somewhere where I can't keep an eye on him. You head toward the canyon that brought us here and I'll check the other side of this here valley. Pedro, you stay put. If Cuchillo returns make damn sure he don't leave. Jones, if you see him, plug him. It's what you've been itching to do anyway. He's making me nervous."

"I thought you said you needed that old Injun to lead you to Cochise's bones."

"I don't need him that bad. Cuchillo ain't gonna tell us nothin', and besides, give us a week or two of searching and we will find that hidden burial ground by ourselves. If we don't"—Sargot shrugged his shoulders—"then we don't. Just the same, I don't care to have that Indian around any longer."

Jones smiled broadly. "It'll be a pleasure to plug him for you, Jake." He started away then turned back and said to Pedro, "Hey, don't you go drinking up all that whiskey on us, hear?"

"He won't drink it all," Sargot said. "Bad manners or not, some things are just worth killing over."

Cuchillo stayed with the shadows and moved eastward along the base of the escarpment. Already he was aware of the movement out in the valley, but there was a place he had to get to, a place he remembered that was in the mouth of the canyon; a place where he could wait out the night in safety, and that meant breaking across the open where faint moonlight showed against the curving rise of the canyon.

His ears heard the approaching footsteps, measured the strides; too long for Pedro, too light to be the bearded one . . . Cuchillo paused and a smile curved his lips. It was the skinny one—the one called Jones. Cuchillo's fingers wrapped about the hilt of his long hunting knife, and he merged soundlessly with the tangled vegetation growing up at the escarpment's roots; waiting as Jones appeared from the darkness.

Ben Jones crashed through the weeds like a wounded bull elk, passed within a few feet of Cuchillo's waiting blade and then turned his back on it to peer out into the valley.

"Damned Injun," he whispered to himself.

Cuchillo leaned toward him and a single lunge would end it all for Jones. For an instant the messenger of death hovered over him in indecision. Nothing would be more satisfying to the old man than to plunge his blade into this skinny one's back or rip open his throat and feel the warm blood spilling out onto his hands—but not now, he told himself, pulling back. All things in their time and for to-night he would allow Jones to live . . . a little while longer.

"To hell with him—to hell with that fat ass Sargot as well," Jones said aloud. "I'm going back to get me some whiskey," and he crashed back out of the weeds toward the fire flickering in the distance. In a moment darkness swal-lowed him up and Cuchillo stepped out of his cover, listen-ing to his receding footsteps until they were no more.

He started along the escarpment once again, somewhat

annoyed at himself for allowing Jones to escape death so easily. He countered this self-incrimination with the comforting fact that the steps he was now taking were no longer completely of his own doing—they were being ordered by some force which he would admit he knew very little of. Since leaving the burial grounds and his wife's side, he'd been driven as if by a force greater than himself, and for now he could but only obey its unspoken commands.

At the canyon's mouth Cuchillo sprinted across the open space touched by moonlight and climbed up into a niche in the rocks which, in the past, had secreted Apache braves as a last line of defense in guarding the valley's entrance. Now he was safe and could rest until morning—until *he* came. Restlessness stirred within his bones and the heat of impending battle brought a rush of blood to his face. His eyes smiled. They were the eyes of an old man who had much to look forward to in the next few hours. With these thoughts he closed them and entertained a vision of Sun Rising until sleep overtook him.

"Nope, I ain't going to do it," Jemima said, crossing her arms in defiance.

Kendell tugged the cinch tight, turned and faced the little girl. "I'll hog-tie you if that's what it will take."

"You won't do that either," she answered him confidently.

"Oh, you don't think so?"

"No, I don't. We'd be in a lot more danger tied up here alone, where animals and who knows what else could get us, than riding into that canyon with you."

He was frowning again aware that he was about to lose another argument to Jemima. The unfortunate thing was, as before, she was absolutely right. Now she was seeing clean through his bluff. He slid his Winchester into the saddle scabbard and said, "I don't know what trouble I'm going to run into in there. They have guns and no reluctance in using them. I probably won't be coming out of there again. It's a cinch if I don't then you and Willie won't, either."

"You weren't so worried about us a couple of days ago."

"That was a couple days ago."

"So, what changed?"

"You and Willie aren't coming along and that's all there is to it."

"Yes we are and you can't stop us. We've come along with you this far; we intend to see it all the way through. Besides, if you leave us out here while you go off and get yourself killed what chance do you think we would have of making our way out of these mountains and across that desert by ourselves? Not much, so I think we better take our chances with you."

"You keep saying *we.* Does Willie feel the same way about this as you do?"

Willie stammered, saying, "I . . . I don't want you to leave us out here alone, Mister Kendell. I want to go with you."

Kendell returned his attention to the bedroll, tying it up behind the cantle. He said, without looking at her, "It seems as though I find myself outnumbered."

"Does that mean you'll let us come along?"

"Well, I reckon if I can't hog-tie you and leave you here

because all the wild animals that roam these hills might gobble you up, and if you don't intend to stay here under your own free will, then I haven't got much choice left me. After all, I'd hate to feel responsible for you and your brother becoming the main course in some dangerous, wild kangaroo rat's dinner."

Jemima frowned.

He turned back toward her. "You can come along, little one, but under one condition. Once we are under way you and your brother obey me explicitly. I mean to the letter. If I say jump, I want to see two pairs of little feet treading air —got it?"

"Yes, sir."

Although he admired her for her spunk, his expression remained stoic, and he studied her closely, trying to recall that timid little girl he had picked up only three days before. Somewhere along the way she had changed places with this young free spirit. She had changed, as most people tend to do, and he couldn't help thinking it was for the better. Being timid did not get a person very far in this hard world, and Kendell had a notion that little Jemima Butler was almost ready to take hold of this old world by the tail. Well, as far as he was concerned she was welcome to it and he wasn't so sure the world would not be a better place for it.

Kendell readied the children's horses then gave the Indian a hand up to his feet. Earlier, in the predawn hours, the Apache had protested when Kendell had explained to him what he wanted him to do, but despite his hate and his fear of the evil spirits that supposedly haunted Cochise's stronghold, he readily agreed to comply. His hate and fear were not quite strong enough to resist persuasion of the proper kind—the kind of persuasion a large-bore revolver has.

He rose to his feet reluctantly and, with a hard, dark eye turned narrowly to the gun in Kendell's hand, started on foot into the rocky labyrinth.

21

The sun climbed slowly above the valley's irregular rim. For an hour Juana had laid upon the grass with her eyes open, unable to sleep, dreading its arrival, and now it was here, the time had come and she knew she could no longer put off the thing which they had to do.

Teresa and Olinda were still asleep. How could they sleep knowing what had to be done? *Sleep!* If only she could fall asleep and wake up from this terrible nightmare to the sounds of her mother fixing breakfast and her father sharpening his plow upon the wheel—if only . . . but this line of thinking would do her no good now.

A short distance away the *pigs* snorted in their drunken sleep. The fire had gone out and a strong, smoldering odor hung in the quiet air—quiet enough for her to hear their breathing. Ah, their breathing, she thought, it was that breathing that she would have to bring to a stop this morning. But would she be up to the task . . . ?

She would! she told herself firmly, sitting up.

"Teresa," she whispered, gently prodding the other's shoulder. "Teresa, wake up."

Teresa came awake, looking at Juana, all at once remembering what this morning meant. She pushed herself up, rubbing the sleep from her eyes.

"Is it time?"

"In a little while, when they wake up."

Teresa nodded her head toward Olinda. "Then we should let her sleep a little longer. The sleep will keep the pain of it from her a few more moments. We can at least give her that."

"Yes. The less time she has to dwell on what must be done, the better it will be for all of us."

Teresa said softly, "I pray to God that if he permits any of us to live through this morning that it will be Olinda. She is too good a person to die in a place like this."

"We will not die," Juana said, with a hardness in her voice. She stared at the three sleeping men. "They will die."

"How are we going to do this?" Teresa asked.

Juana gave a slight shrug of her shoulder. "I am not certain exactly how it will all go," she said, "a lot will depend on them. We will just have to wait and see. After they wake up Sargot will either come for me or he will not. If he does not, well, then I must go to him." She could not avoid the tone of disgust which crept into her words.

"And we to them," Teresa added.

Juana nodded her head slowly.

Teresa gripped her arms, hugging herself. "Well, one way or the other it will all be over within a few more hours."

"Do not be so morose, Teresa."

She laughed quietly. "Morose? No, not that, just realistic. I have held my tongue about this escapade for Olinda's sake, but to you I can say what I think, and what I think is that this plan of yours treads very near to suicide . . . wipe that petulant look from your face, you know it is true."

Juana struggled with her temper. "I believe it was you who said she would rather die attempting escape than to die and not have tried anything at all, or something to that effect."

"Yes, I said that, and I meant it. It is the only reason I am going along with this dangerous scheme of yours. It may be foolhardy and it may be suicidal, but it is something to do, and unfortunately, it is the best we can come up with under these circumstances."

"Then I want to hear no more talk of failure or suicide."

Olinda's voice cut in. "What are you two whispering about? What were you saying about suicide?" She rose, resting on her elbows and looking at them, then sat straight up yawning and rubbing her eyes.

Juana and Teresa came about in unison and looked at her. Juana stammered but Teresa cut her off, saying, "I had said I wished those pigs would commit suicide. It would save us much trouble."

Olinda was not amused. "I am afraid there is not much chance of that happening," she said dryly, shaking her head.

"Yes, Juana said as much herself."

Changing subjects, Juana said, "I am getting hungry."

"How can you think of food?"

She looked at Olinda. "I do not have to think about it; my stomach keeps me reminded."

"Well, I suppose I am hungry, too," Olinda said, frowning, "only there is not much chance of getting anything to eat, not until *they* wake up. Considering all that whiskey they drank last night, that could be hours."

Olinda's words shot through the two girls like a lightning bolt. All at once Juana and Teresa looked at each other, struck with the same thought.

"Do you think . . . ?" Teresa said, suddenly breathless.

Juana was nodding her head. "Of course, it is perfect! Even now it is the whiskey that is making them sleep this late." She glanced up at the sun. The valley was bright and warming and Juana was certain it was the whiskey in their blood making them sleep on. Even Pedro, who had been assigned the task of guarding them, was fast asleep.

Olinda was confused. "What are you two talking about?" she demanded.

Hope had suddenly replaced the gloom. Juana said, "You are brilliant, Olinda!" and she hugged the surprised girl.

"Me?"

"Yes, you!"

"But . . . ?"

"We were too blind to see the opportunity the Lord placed right before our eyes. Listen, we must work fast, before they wake up."

"Work fast? Work fast at what?"

"Olinda, you are too dense-headed this morning. We'll use the same plan as before, only we change the beginning a little. That should be to your liking, Olinda, as well as ours. We have to get their weapons away from them while they still sleep, and if we are stealthful enough, and they continue snoring like old cows, we will see to it that they never wake up again."

Then Olinda understood, and a look of horror came into her eyes. "Kill them while they sleep!"

"Asleep or awake, what difference should it make?" Juana said irritably.

Olinda shook her head. "But that will be plain out and out murder."

"We went all through this before, Olinda. We had decided that killing a crazed animal is not murder. You had agreed, remember?"

"Yes, I remember, but the circumstances were different. The way we had it all worked out it would be more like self-defense than outright murder."

Teresa threw up her hands in disgust. "Forget it, Olinda, stay here. Juana and I will take care of this ourselves if you have no stomach for it."

"No . . . no, I am involved too; I will carry my share of it."

"Are you certain you will be able to?" Juana asked, studying her closely. "Because if you have any doubts, then stay back here. A moment's indecision will get you and the rest of us killed. As Teresa has said, we can handle it by ourselves. All we need to do is get one of their guns in our hands. I for one do not mind killing a sleeping devil."

"No, I will do it. It's just that it is going to take me a moment to readjust my thinking on it."

"We do not have a moment to waste."

"All right, all right, then let's do it. Let's do it now and be done with it," Olinda said.

Juana glanced questioningly at Teresa, seeing the hardness in her eyes. She would carry out her end of it. Olinda still had that wide look of a person trying to sort things out in her own head. It made Juana uneasy. She said to them, "Just like we planned it before. Teresa, you take Pedro. Olinda, you must kill Jones . . . and I will kill the leader pig. Now, we must be quiet, and we must not make any mistakes, or allow fear to get its grip on us." She looked at Olinda with these words.

"One other thing. Once we leave here to do it, it must be completed. We will be committed, there will be no turning back, and if they should wake up and we fail to kill even one of them, it will certainly mean our own deaths. Is that clearly understood?"

Juana waited while the girls each mumbled their agreements. She drew a breath and said, "Then let's do it."

They rose to their feet and started toward the sleeping men. As they approached Juana threw Teresa a sideways glance, catching the other's eye. When she had her attention she shifted her view to Olinda's back and silently formed the words, *watch her.*

Teresa understood and nodded her head. They both knew Olinda was the weak link in their chain and in all probability it would be up to one of them to finish Jones off if Olinda were to suddenly freeze up on them.

As Juana moved, the sound of the soft grass crushing beneath her feet seemed extraordinarily loud, and even the light rustling of her clothes threatened to give them away—or, at least it sounded so to her ears. She found that she was breathing rapidly and she made an effort to get it under control, drawing in deep breaths, letting them out slowly, taking with them some of the tension building up inside her like steam in a locomotive.

The three separated, each heading for her own target. Juana tossed a quick glance at the other girls. Teresa had stopped a foot or two from Pedro and was looking back at Juana. Olinda came up short, pausing by the sleeping form of Ben Jones. And then Juana herself was standing over the sleeping Jake Sargot. Her heart raced. He was snoring loudly, breathing unevenly. Last night's dinner still clung to his filthy beard in places, and he reeked with the odor of sweat. Even though there was plenty of water about, Sargot had chosen not to use any of it except to drink occasionally. Standing near to such a man was repulsive enough, but enduring his horrid body against hers was now unbearable. Juana's brain reeled at the thought, and then she got control of herself again. What she had to do now required clear thinking. Carefully her dark eyes searched for his gun.

Her heart sank when she saw his huge right arm resting atop the holster belt. There was always the little gun in his boot, she thought, but it would be all but impossible to remove the derringer without waking him, so the six-shooter was her only possibility. She held her breath, steadied herself and quietly lowered herself to the grass by his side. A glance told her both Teresa and Olinda were making their move cautiously also. Juana put them out of mind. Concentrate, she told herself, as her fingers inched toward the pistol butt protruding from under Sargot's arm.

In her mind she went over the procedure. Guns were not a common item in Juana's life, but she was not totally ignorant of them, either. The hammer would have to be drawn all the way back before she could pull the trigger. She knew that much. She knew cocking the hammer would rotate the cylinder, and that would make a loud clicking noise before it finally locked in place with a fresh round lined up with the barrel and the firing pin poised above it. That noise, the noise of the cylinder, would surely wake Sargot and she knew she would have to be quick about it; she would have to cock the gun and pull the trigger all in one speedy motion before he became aware of what was happening.

Her fingers froze in midmotion when Sargot snorted and

worked his cracked lips in his sleep. He smelled of whiskey mingled with sweat and it turned her stomach, but her eyes remained locked on his face until he settled down again to his irregular breathing.

Another glance told her Olinda was already reaching for Ben Jones' weapon. Juana's heart raced. Olinda was having some difficulty getting at the gun. The apprehension forced her to look away. She felt easier watching Teresa's slow, steady progress; carefully sliding the rifle from its scabbard on the saddle where Pedro's head was resting. Juana could do nothing to help Olinda now and she turned her attention back to the task before her, starting her hand toward Sargot's pistol again. In a moment her fingers wrapped around the gun.

A horrible noise brought her head around. All at once Olinda let out a chilling scream that turned Juana's blood to ice. Olinda staggered away from Jones, her hands clutching at her stomach. Then she turned and fell backward.

In desperation Juana jerked the gun from Sargot's holster but a hand came up, caught her by the throat and threw her to the ground. Sargot's face reared up, ugly, staring into hers. Behind her a rifle shot went off followed by the sounds of struggling—sounds instantly drowned out by the rattle of her own teeth as Sargot's fist crashed into her jaw.

Jake Sargot stood and glared down at the crumpled girl at his feet. Jones knelt over Olinda and yanked the broad knife from her body, grinning up at Sargot.

"The fumbling little bitch was trying to get at my pistol," he said, wiping the blood from the knife with Olinda's skirt.

"Is she dead?"

"Naw, not yet. There is a lot of pain left in that gut

wound before it finally does her in. Yep, a whole lot of pain," and Ben Jones was smiling broadly, watching Olinda turning in torment.

Pedro had Teresa on the ground, straddling the girl who was kicking and fighting like a green-broke mare. He wrestled the rifle out of her hands and pressed the barrel of it into her throat.

"You all right, Pedro?"

He glanced up quickly. "Dammit, give me a hand here!" he said.

Sargot motioned to Ben Jones. Jones slugged Teresa, whose body went limp.

"I'm truly surprised at you, Pedro," Jones chided. "A wisp of a girl like that and you need my help to handle her."

"Shut up!" He stuck up a bloodied hand. "The bitch shot me! She shot me with my own rifle, dammit!"

"Well, I'd say you were damned lucky she wasn't a better shot," Sargot said unsympathetically.

Pedro got to his feet, breathless. "Too bad they had to try that," he said. "Damn! I didn't want to kill 'em."

"I warned them. They all knew the cost of trying to escape." Sargot looked at Pedro. "We don't need their kind of trouble anyway. Kill her."

He turned back to Juana. She had regained enough of her senses to understand completely the meaning of that hard look on his face. It was over now, she knew; her plan had gotten them all killed. The thought of dying didn't really alarm her. Sargot stopped and aimed his gun. As he drew back the hammer of his pistol, Juana was ready for death. The prayer on her lips was that it would come swiftly and that, beyond this life, there would truly be the great peace the priest used to speak of . . .

And then in the corner of her eye a movement caught her attention and she turned for a better look; what she saw made her eyes grow even wider than the pistol aimed at her head had.

22

Cuchillo had come awake some time earlier, hearing the sounds of morning all around him, but listening for one sound in particular. If he ever had any doubts concerning his intuitions in the past, he did not have them now.

It was a whisper on the Devil's Wind that first alerted him of their coming. And then later, when the sun was fully up and the little niche behind the rocks warming from its heat, he heard the sounds he had been waiting for. Distant at first, the scraping of iron against rock echoing from far down the canyon. That was all—horses, laden with riders, picking their way slowly up the canyon. In his heart Cuchillo knew a certain urgency, but he did not understand the reason for it; where had it come from and what were the spirits trying to tell him? He did not know, but the feeling was there just the same and he grew anxious.

He stayed hidden in his place long enough to see them come around the bend in the canyon. He recognized him at once. So, this was the devil who had followed them across the burning sands, who had followed the faint trail Cuchillo had left behind in the river canyon—and it did not surprise him either. Watching Matt Kendell, Cuchillo thought how very different he looked from when he had last seen him by the well in San Pablo. Well, what had happened there would change most strong men, he knew. Change the strong ones and kill the weak.

He turned his attention to the young Apache striding ahead of them. His hands were tied behind him and the end of the long rope was wrapped around Kendell's saddle horn. Behind them rode two small children. Cuchillo recalled the smoke he had seen climbing off the desert floor. He had known its meaning at the time, and now, seeing the Apache and the children, he did not have to be told what had transpired.

Looking back at Kendell, Cuchillo was aware of a certain feeling of respect for him. He was like the Apache, he thought, but more than that, he had the tenacity of the Devil. He knew this man was more than an equal match for the three men in the valley.

He stayed in his place, watching them approach until they came to a stop below him. Then he knew it was time for him to leave, still conscious of that nagging anxiety he could not explain. Following a narrow declivity, Cuchillo climbed to the ridgetop above the valley and paused to look out across his valley. His old eyes were attracted by movement down below and at once he understood what it was that was bothering him. The three women had gone ahead with their plan—their deadly plan, but they were too soon. If they had only waited a little while longer. He did not care to see them die, but now it was too late for him to do anything about it.

Cuchillo lowered himself over the rim of the valley and with the toe of his moccasin he probed for something on the sheer rock wall. In a moment he found the little hole there and slowly he began his descent, employing the hand and toe holes which had been carved into the living rock. He did not know the people who had carved them, or where they had come from or where they had gone. Only that this way down into the valley was ancient and had already been a well-worn path by the time his people had moved into the valley. The handiwork of some previous inhabitors. Some tribe long dead, which had fought the land as the Apaches had done—fought it and lost . . .

The Indian stopped and pointed a finger at the place where the canyon took a turn. "It is there," he said, clearly not anxious to go any farther.

Trouble was in the air like the electricity of a lightning storm. "Sit down over there," Kendell ordered, swinging out of his saddle. "You two stay put," he said to the children.

Jemima and Willie sat obediently upon their animals while Kendell tied the Indian's legs with the remaining length of rope and sat him against the rocky wall.

"What do you want me and Willie to do, Mister Kendell?"

"You think you can find your way out of here by yourselves?"

Jemima nodded her head.

"All right, then listen closely to what I have to say. I'm going in there and I don't know if I'm going to come walking out again."

"You will, Mister Kendell, you will. I just know it."

He smiled at Willie. "Well, I appreciate your confidence, son, but just in case I don't, this is what I want you to do—" He glanced up at the morning sun, low in the east. "If I am not back here by the time that sun is straight overhead I want the two of you to ride out of here. Take it careful and you'll find your way out all right." He removed the water bag from his saddle along with the canteen and handed them up to the kids.

"Take these. There is enough water left to get you down to the stream we passed. Water your horses well. Fill the bags. They will last the two of you four or five days; you won't be needing any more than that. Once you are on the desert head due north. You'll know you're going north by watching your shadow. It will be following you on the left side until noon, and then it will move across to your right. Do you understand?"

"Yes, sir," Jemima said, not thrilled with the idea.

"Say it back to me."

She sighed as if all this was unnecessary. "Shadow on our left until noon—that's when the sun is straight overhead," she added, thoroughly unimpressed with Kendell's attempt at explaining rudimentary navigation. "Then we look for our shadows on our right side. That way we will always be heading north . . . more or less."

He couldn't help grinning at her. "More or less," he said. "Now, in about three days you will come to a river—well, it isn't much of a river this time of the year, but you will recognize it for what it is. The water dips under the sand mostly, but in low places it breaks the surface, forming little pools—you'll know. When you get there look for a small ridge of hills that look as if someone took a saw to them, cutting the tops flat. They will either be to the east or the west, depending on how close you stayed to a northern course. In any case, you need to follow the river toward those flattopped hills. When you come in line with them, San Pablo should be clearly in sight. Go there, seek out a man named Onesimo—Onesimo Gutiérrez. He's a good man; he'll help you. Tell him who you are, tell him I sent you. You got all of that?"

"Yes, sir, but . . ."

"But what?"

"But what about you?"

He frowned at her. "If I'm not out of there by noon, then I'm never coming out. You two will be on your own, it's just as plain as all that. You will have to get your brother and yourself out of here and you will have to do it alone. I've given you all the help I can. You have your pa's rifle and all the water you will need. With any luck you will make it all right. San Pablo is the nearest place where you can get help."

Jemima studied him a moment then turned her face away from him. "I want you to come back," she said softly, wiping something from her eye, then looking back at him.

"I want to come back, too," he answered her gently, realizing that for the first time since the death of María he really felt like living on. Looking briefly at Jemima and Willie, Kendell knew there was still much to live for. Turning away, he swung back onto the saddle and checked the load in his Winchester, cradling the rifle in his arm.

"What should I do about him?" Jemima asked, indicating the Apache trussed up in the shade of the canyon walls.

"Leave him be. It will take some time, but he'll cut through those ropes using the rocks. He'll be all right. Don't worry about him, think only of yourself and getting to San Pablo. That is all that is important to you now."

"Yes, sir."

Kendell started his horse toward the valley entrance then

stopped short and turned in his saddle. "One more thing, Jemima. I don't want you or your brother sticking your nose outside this canyon to see what's going on out there. No matter how much shooting you hear, you stay put right here. You got that straight?"

Jemima pouted and stretched an arm behind her to scratch her back. "I got it," she said reluctantly, and crossed the fingers of her hidden hand.

The distant, echoing sound of a gunshot rang from the valley. It wasn't the sharp crack of a pistol, but the heavier percussion of a rifle going off.

Matt Kendell swung around, then looked back at Jemima one more time. "Remember what I told you," he said, then spurred his horse forward.

The canyon made a bend before it opened up to spill out onto the green valley. The grass was deep. It encircled a small pond at the center, and by that pond he saw them; without seeing their faces, he recognized each one. The heavy one . . . the Mexican . . . *the skinny one!*

It was he, the one who had murdered María, who now stood over the body on the ground. He said something to the Mexican. Then the big one turned away from them to stand over the other girl, also on the ground. Kendell saw the gun come up in his hand.

He observed all this in the brief moments it took his horse to gallop wildly across the green valley. Dropping reins across the saddle horn, he threw his rifle to his shoulder.

Juana saw the movement, turned toward it and at once recognized the rider who bore down on them. Her eyes popped as if seeing a ghost.

"Padre!" she whispered, but it could have just as well been a shout of surprise, and Sargot, hearing the pounding hooves behind him now, spun around.

This rider coming toward him was putting a rifle to his shoulder. Sargot snapped his gun up and fired. Kendell's rifle spoke too and both bullets went wide of their mark.

Riding in amongst them, Kendell swung the rifle. Pedro struggled to raise his rifle, but like a mule kick out of the dark, Kendell sent him sprawling, then directed his charging animal toward Ben Jones. Jones scrambled out of the way and for the moment Kendell ignored him, swinging his horse at Sargot.

The gun in Sargot's hand rose about the same time Juana's foot slammed into his shin, and he hobbled backward howling. Kendell leaped from his saddle.

They crashed to the ground, Kendell atop Sargot, and the impact took the wind from the bearded man. But he recovered quickly and the two men tumbled across the grass.

Jones moved back in, pistol drawn, waiting for an opening.

Sargot connected with a solid punch and rolled out from under Kendell's hands. Kendell struck back, grabbed a hank of chin hair and together they lurched down toward the pond.

Jones hopped out of their way, waiting for a clear shot. His hungry eyes gleamed and his hands sweated in anticipation on the grip of the pistol.

Teresa's eyes fluttered open to the blue of the sky overhead, then she heard the sounds of struggling to her side. Pushing herself up, she glanced at Juana, sitting some distance away. Looking farther, she saw the two men down by the pond and all at once she recognized Kendell.

"My God!" she said, looking again at Juana in confusion.

Between the two girls lay Olinda. Teresa slipped the rifle from Pedro's fingers and crawled to her side. Olinda's chest heaved as she fought for breath.

"Olinda," she said, sliding an arm under the girl's head. Olinda's eyes rolled toward her; wide eyes that stared through a glazing of tears. They looked at Teresa a long moment before flickering away to view Juana as she crawled up beside her.

"I . . . I did not do it very well, Juana, did I?" she said weakly. "I'm sorry."

"Hush, do not speak now."

"I must. I must talk to someone before I . . . I die."

Juana glanced up at Teresa and then across to the two men locked in combat. She said to Olinda, "Don't waste your strength talking to us. Hold on to life a little longer and I will get the priest for you."

"But . . ."

"Do not talk," Juana said sternly and left her, snatching up Sargot's pistol from where it had fallen on the ground.

Kendell rolled from a punch and came up with a fist that sent Sargot staggering backward. Kendell moved in, hit the bigger man again, aware of a warm dampness spreading across his side.

Sargot threw up an arm to block and swung out, clipping him across the chin. It stunned Kendell for an instant and then he came out of it moving catlike to avoid the other fist that sliced the air alongside his head.

Ben Jones danced around them with his gun ready, and

then the break he had been waiting for came. Kendell and Sargot parted just long enough to suck in a breath of air, but it was all the opportunity Jones needed and he swung his gun toward Kendell.

From out of nowhere a knife flickered in the morning sunlight and before Jones could pull the trigger the knife point split his sternum in two, sliding in until it finally came to rest upon his spine.

His mouth gasped open but there wasn't enough life left in him to emit a cry, and as he turned around with staring eyes and his legs falling out from under him he saw the smile that spread unembarrassedly across Cuchillo's face. Jones died before he hit the ground, but in death a spasm in his finger tugged back on the trigger and the gun in his hand went off in Cuchillo's belly.

The gunshot turned Kendell's head and then Sargot was on top of him. The fight took them back up toward the dead campfire where Juana waited for her turn, with the pistol gripped firmly in her small hand.

Kendell was breathing heavy. The wear and abuse of the past week were beginning to show now and the bigger man's weight was swaying the advantage. He knew he could take Sargot if he could keep some distance between them, striking and dancing back out of the way of his blows, but like this, fighting his weight as well as his muscle, in his weakened condition, he was losing ground quickly.

But Jake Sargot was having difficulty, too. The battle was going his way, but the victory was not coming easy. On top for the moment, he reared back an arm. Kendell jabbed a knee into his side. Sargot tumbled and Kendell rolled over, throwing two quick jabs which broke Sargot's nose and brought forth a gusher of blood. It ran into his eyes and spilled down his throat, choking him. Coughing, Sargot tried to protect his face while Kendell moved in with another volley. Sargot's hand swept up, catching his fist, and for a while they struggled that way, muscle against muscle.

Then Sargot saw the gun in Kendell's holster and reached for it, tugging it free and cocking the hammer at the same time. Instantly Kendell grabbed at the gun. Sargot used his greater weight to roll Kendell off him and as they turned the gun went off. The report was a low thud, muffled by their bodies.

For a long moment neither of them moved and Juana stood watching in horror, her gun ready and not knowing quite what to do. Then, with little strength left, Kendell rolled Sargot's heavy body off him.

"Padre!" Juana cried, kneeling down beside him and helping him sit up. "Padre, are you all right?"

Gulping in short breaths, Kendell nodded his head.

Juana stared at him, but it wasn't a ghost, it was living flesh and blood she saw. Yet Teresa had said the Father was dead, that he had been killed. She had seen him killed—or at least she thought she had, for here he was. It was truly a miracle!

Still, Juana questioned her eyes. This man looked like Father Kendell and yet he was different. She had never seen him dressed in anything other than his long brown robes. His face had always been smooth and clean-shaven, his eyes gentle and soft. Now he was filthy, with a week's growth on his chin already darkening into the beginnings of a full beard, and his eyes—it was his eyes that frightened her now, hard and ablaze with a fire she had never seen in them before.

She stared down at his bloodied shirt. "You have been injured, Father."

For some reason her addressing him as "Father" sounded foreign to his ears, and that surprised Kendell. It had been only a week since he had given up the role of village priest and he figured it should take more time than that to get all those years out of his system.

He said to Juana, "I am all right, but you, you and Teresa and Olinda . . ." Then his eyes fell upon the girl on the ground. "Olinda—?"

"Father, she needs you. I fear she is dying."

Kendell stood painfully and gazed briefly down at Sargot. He was drawn up in pain, breathing raggedly. Ben Jones' eyes were gaping in death, a knife sticking out of his skinny chest. Kendell's eyes lingered upon Jones' lifeless body, allowing the hate he had known for the man to ebb slowly away. *An eye for an eye—a life for a life,* he found himself thinking, recalling María's playful smile, a smile that would haunt him for the rest of his life.

Turning away, he noted the Apache there too, his black eyes open, watching him. The old man was breathing shallowly and he seemed not anxious, but truly at peace, content to wait for death. A little way away the Mexican was lying unconscious where the swinging butt of his rifle had sent him sprawling.

Kendell knelt beside Olinda. Her eyes moved toward him then opened.

"Father," she said, "you have come at last. I knew you

would. Teresa said you had been killed, but I knew you were not. God has sent you."

"Do not talk, my child," he said gently.

"But I must. I must give you my confession before I die."

"It is not necessary, Olinda," he said, while making the sign of the cross over her. "I have absolved you of your sins in the name of the Father and the Son and the Holy Ghost," he went on, feeling suddenly very hypocritical thinking of his own sins of the last week. Who would absolve him? But he went through the ritual just the same—for Olinda's sake, knowing that his words made little difference as far as her eternal life was concerned.

Well, it had been a lesson hard learned, and he figured he could never go back to what he had been, but that didn't mean he could not go back at all. In a sense these were indeed his people. They looked up to him for guidance and he had no right deserting them—well, maybe he did have the right; after all, it was his own life to live as he pleased, but in San Pablo it had not been such a bad life.

When he had finished, a look of peace spread across Olinda's face. She could die now assured of her entrance into heaven.

"Father," she wheezed, "Father, tell my mother and my father that I loved them . . . please."

"I will."

She smiled and then she said, "Are they all dead? They were evil men, Father, but in my heart I have forgiven them. My soul is free from hate and I can enter into God's Kingdom now with no shame."

Kendell said nothing, but thought of his own guilt. Behind him he heard Juana's low sobbing. It was too bad, but it was true, the good always did seem to die young. He seemed to recall that he and Jemima had had a conversation along those lines too.

Olinda smiled up at him and her smile suddenly turned hard and her eyes lost their life. It was a strange thing and it reminded him of the death he had once witnessed on Virginia battlefields long ago.

He lowered her head gently to the ground and placed a consoling hand upon Juana's shoulder. Looking at Teresa, he asked, "Are you going to be all right?"

"Yes, Father," she said softly.

Turning, Juana said, "Father, the Indian befriended us; perhaps you should go to him."

Kendell squatted on his heels beside the old man. It was a bad wound and it would not be long now. He knew it and so did Cuchillo.

"Thank you for helping them," Kendell said.

"They are strong women. The Apache admires strength. You are a strong man; I knew it was you who was coming. You fought not only these men, but the devil inside of you, and you have won both battles. Now I feel the devil fleeing from you. Indeed, you have a mighty and powerful God, as I told you once before by the well."

Kendell said nothing to this, but asked, "Is there something I can do for you? Someone I can tell?"

Cuchillo smiled at this. "I have no one who will miss me. All those who I care about are right here in this valley with me. They are drawing near to me even now. But there is one thing"—he paused, then continued—"I would like to be laid with my people, in the sacred place."

"Of course. Where is this place?"

Cuchillo raised a shaking finger and pointed at the narrow slash of a shadow across the valley wall. "Up there. You will find a cave; beyond is where my people lie."

"Yes, I will do this for you."

"Good," Cuchillo said with his last breath before he let go of his life and died.

The valley was somber with the quietness of death and Kendell stood up. He had had more than his share of killing and what he wanted now was to be by himself for a moment. He had but turned his back when Juana cried out. He swung around to see a shining derringer in Sargot's hand pressing against her temple.

"You should not have left me for dead," Sargot wheezed. "That was a mistake, the last mistake you'll ever make. Drop that gun and step away from it."

Kendell let the six-shooter slip from his fingers.

Sargot said, "Well, if it ain't the priest from San Pablo. You're the last person I expected to show up. I thought Jones got rid of you. You don't look much like a priest dressed like that, don't act like one either."

"Let the girl go."

"I told them that I'd kill 'em if they tried to escape, and that's just what I intend to do. And after them, you."

Sargot grabbed his six-shooter out of Juana's hand, shoving the little derringer into his pocket.

"What good will killing us do you? You're dying."

"Hell, priest, I've lived through worse than this; I'll make it all right."

Kendell dared not move. Maybe he could take Sargot, stop him from killing all three of them . . . maybe, but now even one more death would be unacceptable.

"You're bleeding like a stuck pig. Five minutes from now you won't be able to move. You'll lie there and bleed to death."

"Maybe so, maybe five minutes is all I got, but that's more time than I need, and a sight longer than the three of you have." He turned the gun toward Teresa.

"Mister," a small voice spoke from behind. Kendell went rigid as he heard the horse come to a halt behind him.

Sargot's head jerked about. "What the hell? Where'd the kid come from?"

Kendell's heart sank. He had told Jemima to stay put. *He had told her, dammit!* If anything at all, he wanted to preserve her life, and now here she was, riding in bold as new brass.

Kendell shot a hard glance at the girl, but Jemima ignored him, her eyes fixed on Sargot.

"Mister, I can make you a deal if you let them go."

"You got grit, girl," he answered, "but I ain't interested in no deal you can make me."

"Why don't you listen to it before you make up your mind."

Jemima glanced at the pile of gold cups off to the side. There were other items there too, things she did not recognize, but she knew this was what they had stolen from the church in San Pablo, the stuff Kendell had told her and Willie about.

Looking back at Sargot, she said, "It appears you have a fondness for gold, mister. I got some more gold for you; you care to see it?"

Sargot's face changed a little, becoming wary. "You got gold?"

Jemima showed him the two pouches of coins which they had taken from Annie's sack. "I'd say there was near a thousand dollars here, mister. It will be a whole lot easier to spend, and draw a lot less questions than all that other stuff over there. If you do make it out of here, you are going to need some ready cash, aren't you?"

"You're a pretty smart kid. Gimme here, let me see what you got to bargain with."

Jemima tossed the two pouches to him and they fell short a half dozen feet. Sargot leveled his pistol at Juana, pushing himself out along the grass and reaching out for them. When his fingers curled around the pouches Jemima yelled out, *"Willie!"*

Jemima jumped out of her saddle, falling flat to the ground. Kendell had seen this little drama played out once before and knew what was coming next. Diving at Juana, he slammed a shoulder into her, carrying her to the ground as the gun in Sargot's hand went off.

Sargot thumbed back the hammer for a second shot, and then from the ridge came the boom of a rifle. Sargot lurched backward.

Kendell snatched up his six-shooter but Sargot was already dead; a spot of blood over his heart was all that showed. "Well, I'll be damned," Kendell whispered, studying the valley ridge two hundred yards away. He shook his head in amazement as the small figure of a boy stood up with that old Henry rifle clutched in one hand.

"I'll be damned," was all Kendell could say.

Father Matthew Kendell buried Olinda and Cuchillo in the Indians' sacred grounds, and after a short graveside service, he, Jemima, Willie, Juana and Teresa made their way back through the damp cave to the larger valley beyond.

It was a somber company that tramped back to the sparkling pond to finish burying the two other men. Tied hand and foot, Pedro and the Apache sat watching.

They buried the others under the stones that used to surround the Indian campfires of long ago—there were hundreds lying about and it was easier to collect them than to scratch holes in the ground. Afterward, Kendell said a simple prayer over them, although his heart was not in it.

It was dark by the time all this had been accomplished. The next morning Juana did not awake to fear and dread, as she had the day before; instead there was excitement in the air. *They were going home!* Her enthusiasm caught her by surprise and she had to stop and think just why living had meant so little to her only two days before.

Then tears came to her eyes as she thought of Olinda. Olinda had had so much life, so much love, so much hope. Of the three of them, she had been the only one who really cared—and now she was the only one not returning with them. It was sad to think of her alone here after they left—well, she wasn't entirely alone, Juana decided, recalling that Cuchillo had really been a friend of theirs all along. He had looked out for them in his own way, seeing to it they had food and water, and in the end giving his life in their behalf. Olinda would not be entirely alone and that thought made her feel somewhat better.

As the sun climbed higher in the sky, Matt Kendell finished repacking the mule—at least the people of San Pablo would have the religious objects back for their new church, whenever they got around to building one. Kendell snapped the rope taut and drew a knot through as a solemn-faced Willie came over and looked up at him.

"Mister Kendell?"

Kendell could tell something was troubling the boy—and he was pretty sure he knew what it was.

"What do you need, Willie?" he said, tossing a line across the pack and drawing it tight on the other side of the frame.

Willie hesitated a moment and then said, "I did it just like you taught me. I aimed first and was real careful to squeeze the trigger gently. I tried to remember everything and I even braced the rifle on a rock so it wouldn't move. I remembered everything you told me and I didn't take my eyes off the target for a second. When it finally went off—well, it sure took me by surprise."

"You did just fine, Willie. If it wasn't for your fine shooting none of us would have made it. You're something of a hero now."

"Yeah, I know. I did the right thing, except—"

"Except what?" Kendell stooped down by the boy. "You're wondering why, if you did what was right, you are feeling so confused and twisted up inside. Is that it?"

"Gee, Mister Kendell, that's exactly how I'm feeling—how'd you know?"

"Willie, it's never easy to kill another human being—oh, for some folks, like those two we buried over yonder, there is never any feeling of remorse, but that's because their hearts have been dead a long time. Good people, however, people like you and your sister, suffer with the pains that killing brings. The reason is, deep down inside you are so full of life that taking someone else's is like taking away a part of your own life. It's like you're killing a little part of yourself, and that takes a long time to recover from."

"I know what you mean. Gee, I didn't sleep at all last night just thinking about it."

"That's normal. I've spent many a sleepless night myself for the same reason. I reckon I'll have to face a lot more, too, before I get all of this killing out of my system."

"I reckon," Willie repeated solemnly, looking up as Jemima stopped behind him.

The girls had the horses saddled and all that was left for Kendell to do was to help Pedro and the Indian up onto their animals.

"Are the water skins and canteens filled?" he asked.

Juana nodded her head. "Everything is ready, Padre."

He secured the loose ends of the rope to the pack frame then got his two prisoners up onto the horses. Juana came to him then looked out at the pretty little valley.

"Someday I will come back here," she said; "we must not let Olinda think that we have forgotten her."

"Someday you will, Juana, but it is best to give these wounds a long time to heal."

She nodded her head and hugged herself, rubbing at the bumps which suddenly prickled the flesh of her arms.

"Yes, I know. Maybe it will be many years from now, but I will come back."

Kendell said, "No matter where our dead are buried, Juana, they will always remain with us—in here," and he touched his heart.

She smiled at him. "You have always been so wise, Father."

Kendell didn't particularly agree with her on that point

but he saw no reason to dispute it now. Instead he said, "Saddle up, we have a home to return to. A home that needs rebuilding, and shattered lives that can use our help; mothers and fathers who now have no children, and children who now have no mothers and fathers." With these words he looked at Jemima and Willie.

"Come on," he said, "it's about time we start to work on tomorrow."

Matt Kendell swung up into his saddle and took the children home with him.

Douglas Hirt is a writer who lives in Colorado Springs, Colorado. *Devil's Wind* is his first novel. He is currently at work on a sequel and another novel called *A Passage of Seasons.*